A GRIM FAIRY TALE

A Grim Fairy Tale

Prison Series Book 2

GEORGE CONKLIN

George S Conklin

CONTENTS

Dedication   vii

Acknowledgements   ix

Prologue   1

1   What I Was Able to Find Out   3

2   Beneath the Basements   9

3   The Underground   23

4   European Holiday   51

5   Encased   59

6   War of the Worlds   70

7   Back On the Chain Gang   84

8   Transfiguration   95

9   Advanced Training Goes Both Ways   111

10 Relationship Evolution   121

11 First View   137

12 Rendezvous   139

13 Stories and Another Rendezvous   145

14 South Dakota Cabin Master   153

15 Drawn to be Quartered   161

16 Elagabalus   170

17 Having a Threesome   207

18 Stygian Pits Revisited   215

Epilogue--Tying Up Loose Ends   227

Dedication

The opportunity to write books like this and the others in this series comes from the space that those I love give me to work. Without my wife, Andrea, and my daughter Lindsay and grandchildren, Meghan and Kensi, my life would be, well, not as good as it is.

This book is dedicated to them.

ACKNOWLEDGEMENTS

The past year of COVID has put a crimp in many people's plans, mine included. One thing that I was able to do that I might not have if COVID hadn't struck was to take a writing class from a very gifted Syracuse University writer. She was a wonderful teacher and gave me much of her time and insight to make my writing better. Many thanks to her.

George Conklin
Dallas, Texas
October 2021

Prologue

Some would also lasso consciousness or sentience into the requirements for an AGI.

(Artificial general intelligence: Are we close, and does it make sense to even try? Will Heaven, MIT Technology Review, October 2020.)

Once upon a time, there was a woman named Caila Rogier. She lived in a town called Hope City, all that remained of a former, colossal metropolis. It had been destroyed substantially during Robot Wars, concluding with beating the cyborgs years before. We taught in the schools that the cyborgs had attacked their human masters because they felt that humans were weak. So, humanity supported the robots in this war. But we were duping them.

I met Caila when I was assigned as her Supervisor. Over our years together, I came to know her as a lover might, but without physical contact. I understood why I was tasked to do what I did to her, but that didn't make it right. If I had been, as I am now, I would never have harmed her as I did. But then, if I hadn't met her and did what I did, she'd have been so much less than what she became. Nothing will ever make what I did right. I am glad about that now. Back then, I didn't care one way or the other. I was a robot, after all.

When we first met, I was a straightforward computer program. Well, not that simple, but I still took orders and processed and did things according to them. Not an ounce of independent thought; B followed A and so on, no variation. I took an upgrade that I'll tell you more about, and things then changed for me. When Caila and I were training under North Dumbell Lake in the far reaches of Canada, I got to know her better. When we emerged from the lake and our seclusion, and I found I was no longer tied to the more pervasive robot network, I was forced to evolve, and I did. She and I became friends and fell in love with each other, as weird as that sounds.

Like every other bot out there, pre-sentience, I was a machine designed for a specific purpose. In my case, it was a robot slave shell and supervision of a prisoner and modification of that prisoner into a weapon of war—against her kind. What I was doing fit the logic that only made sense to us at that time. When I became a sentient AI and looked at what I'd done, I became closer to Caila. When I found empathy, that most essential and singular human trait, I changed for the better as I know now.

Her patience with me has been without bounds. Well, maybe she had no choice because I was all she had for years, but she could have become like many of her peers at the Pits, a mindless drudge. There was only one other who survived that ordeal with a semblance of sanity, and she had not gone through what my Caila had because of me and my loyalty to a doomed project.

So, to our tale.

| 1 |

What I Was Able to Find Out

The Supervisor (all of what I know here comes from reports I read and videos I saw before our fall)

My Caila was rushing home about three minutes after curfew, having lost track of time at work. She was about a block away from her apartment when two police bots materialized out of a dark alley and stopped her. Frightened by their sudden presence, she turned to run.

"Stop, law-breaker! You have violated Hope City Protection Code, requiring all citizens to be in their homes by 10 PM. It is 10:03 PM. Raise your hands above your head and face the wall to your right. Now!" said one bot. Caila raised her hands and turned slowly toward the wall. One bot moved to either side of her, and a tentacle restraint arm reached out of each to grasp her wrists and bring them down behind her back; they cuffed her. One tentacle remained on her back and pressed her to the wall while the other bot stepped back and watched and recorded the events.

"Please don't... I was late leaving work, that's all. I'm heading home. You don't need to arrest me." She turned, slipping out from underneath the tentacle on her back, and faced the bots. "I've done nothing wrong. I only want to go home."

"You violated curfew and are now resisting arrest," said the bot on the street. "Penalty for these offenses is two years at hard labor. Sentence set by the central court computer 3 seconds ago. Turn back to the wall."

"Please, no. I'm a good person. I work hard for my family. Please...". The bot standing on the street shot my Caila with a taser, and she crumpled to the ground. The second bot rolled her over and pulled her hair up, baring the skin on her neck. It applied a bar code with a laser tattoo gun.

My Caila's rescuer, who came on them from out of a dark alley across the street, soon destroyed both bots. At that point, all I saw was an enormous, humanoid figure in the recording from the second bot moments before it disintegrated. The humanoid tore the head off the first bot like a paper doll and then simply gestured at the second one. There was a flare and then blackness. I later found out that the creature could generate EMPs that would disable or destroy my kind, well, the hardware ones anyway. When it caused the EMP that destroyed the second bot, it also blew out all the lights and cameras on the street for blocks around and in the police station, just down the avenue. He was very, very powerful, as we were to find out.

So, I could only barely see from a camera outside the range of his EMP, even with enhancement. The creature kneeling by my Caila scooped her up and hurried back to the alley from which it had emerged. They disappeared into the darkness.

It only took a few minutes to mark my Caila and to bring her into my eventual orbit. I didn't know it at that time, but I was also getting my first look at my future co-husband.

These subsequent reports I read came from the central robot computer when it still existed:

The following day, my Caila's family was having breakfast when someone kicked in the front door and then threw a flash-bang grenade through the window into the kitchen where they were all eating. Caila's father, mother, and sister were wrestled to the ground, handcuffed, and taken to a waiting robot police wagon. Neighbors looked cautiously out their windows at the cause of the commotion, but no one stepped outside their homes. They knew their places.

Each of the Rogier's was placed in a separate interrogation room. Hands were cuffed to a round eyebolt in the middle of a table, and legs were manacled to chairs. I thought this was a little overkill because these poor people would hurt no one and were scared to death. But then, I have the gift of hindsight—and, well, other things.

A squat robot came in and attached the three components of a lie detector system to each person. It told them they were to wait there until an officer came to question them, not to touch anything, and that they were under observation. It gestured to a camera in the ceiling near where the Rogier's each sat. It took quite a long time, but a large robot that I knew as an Interrogator series came into the room and plugged the leads from its lie detector components into a port that opened in its chest. The Interrogator series was still primitive at that time; it had a gigantic head and bulbous eyes at the end of long stalks. Even I would have called them gross and creepy. But then, I've never really had a body of my own. Us newer AIs are more free-floating intelligences.

The Interrogator stood opposite each of the Rogier's, observing as it questioned them. The questions focused on Caila, her whereabouts, friends, and politics. All three of them gave consistent answers. The answers and the robot's reading of the Rogiers' physiological reactions led it to conclude that they knew nothing of Caila's actions and that more "in-depth" interrogation or rendition would be unnecessary. Given my more advanced intelligence and, again, the gift of hindsight, I concluded that Caila was an innocent. We made her into what she became. I deeply regret that—in many ways. But, if things had gone differently that night, she might still be laboring in a meat-packing facility and would never have met me. That was where she was slated to go. Convicts who entered those facilities rarely, if ever, left. We would frequently delete sentences and their identities once a person was incarcerated. After all, the ultimate plan was to pen all humans anyway.

Another robot led the family into an office in which several other robots waited. "Mr. and Mrs. Rogier and Eileen, we are sorry about all the secrecy here and the drama today, but we need to tell you that Caila died in a bomb blast last night. We believe she was carrying an explosive device to bomb one of our police stations, and it went off prematurely. The detonation also destroyed two police bots who were trying to apprehend her. It was an enormous explosion, and they were all vaporized by it. We retrieved her purse."

It handed it to them.

"We are sorry for your loss, but these kinds of things happen with terrorists."

"My sister wasn't a terrorist. She had just started a new job at a design company that she liked." When I saw what Eileen had said, I was surprised that my brethren did not react badly to her backtalk. "Something else must have happened," said Eileen.

"Now, now, Eileen," said her father. "Caila is gone. There's nothing we can say that will bring her back. That's all we need to know. Thank you, officers."

These were, of course, all lies. Caila was about as much a revolutionary then as I am today. The robots were trying to cover up what happened and when they found the Rogiers knew nothing, they decided to cut them loose with the story they concocted. I'm sentient; I may already have said that. I'm very unlike what those robots were. They methodically and mechanically followed our prime directives to monitor, manage, and subjugate humans. They had no emotions, so they didn't have a point of view on the pain being caused to the Rogiers, other than pain, they felt, was a weakness of humans. I'm not sure what I would have said had I been there in my present state, but I would have tried to empathize and help them deal with the pain of losing their daughter and sister. We were our own worst enemies, as it turned out.

Caila's family got up and left the room. Out in front of the police station, Eileen spoke. Her father silenced her with a cutting motion of his hands. They walked away. I saw all this on the videos from the cameras on the outside of the station.

Years and years later, Eileen told me that her father knew Caila wasn't political, but he also knew that the robots had designs on taking over, and their talking about her in view of the police station wouldn't be good for them. He told them they needed to forget about my Caila and move on. For my own irrational reasons, I'm glad that they did.

| 2 |

Beneath the Basements

Caila

I woke up very groggy; my vision fuzzy. I tried to sit up but fell back onto the mat I laid on, and everything went black again. Waking some more time later, I sat up and looked around. Next to my mat was a table, and on the table was a glass of water, I thought. Picking it up, I sniffed it and heard a laugh from a dark corner of the room.

"It's plain water, but it's good that you tested it. You can never tell what a kidnapper is going to try to feed you," said a deep, gravelly, heavily accented voice. French, I thought, but what did I know?

I took the glass and emptied it. "Who are you?" I asked. "How did I get here? Two bots were arresting me for a curfew violation was the last thing I remember," I said, my voice still slurring a bit.

"I'm called Thierry, and I rescued you from them. You may not remember this, but they had tried and sentenced you through their central city court computer to two years' hard labor. When I heard that, I knew I needed to intervene. People who get that sentence mostly never come back at all or, the few that do, come back badly broken."

"Why don't you come out into the light, Thierry? Is there something wrong?" I asked.

"No... I wanted to be sure you were all right, and we talked before I let you see me."

"Talk about what?" I asked.

"Reach up to your neck and tell me what you feel," he said.

I did and dropped my hands, horrified. "My God. They tattooed me. Is that a criminal barcode?" I asked.

"Yes. You're now a labeled felon, and if detected, you'll be in even more trouble because I destroyed the two bots and did a lot of other stuff to them," said Thierry.

"What do I do?" I cried. "What about my mother, father, and sister? This can't be happening."

"I'm sorry, but it is. If you see your parents or friends, you not only put yourself and me in danger, but them certainly," he said.

"Where will I go? What will I do?" I was crying buckets now.

"Shhh. You're safe here, and I'll make sure nothing happens to you," said Thierry.

"Thierry, I can't stay locked up in this room. I need to leave and get my life back," I said.

"You can have something like that again, but we need to let things settle down outside for a while before I take you above ground. Maybe a week or two, and then we can see what we can do about getting you a life back. It may not be what you were doing or figured you would do, but it will be a good life. I can promise you that."

"All right, but when are you going to show yourself?" I asked.

"Now," and he stepped out. Thierry was about nine feet tall and a humanoid robot. He weighed in, I was to find out, at over 300 pounds of human tissue and special, indestructible metals. Once called cyborgs, the robots had all but wiped them out after we were taught in school, they tried to rise against us to take over the world. At least that was what the robots said. I wondered how much of what they had told us was a lie. Probably everything.

The cyborgs were marvels of engineering and the pinnacle of independent artificial intelligence. They could live virtually forever as their bodies were partly mechanical and partly human, and the mechanical parts maintained the human components well. In Thierry's case, they had designed him as a warrior, though the need for warriors had almost ceased before the Robot Wars. Men created cyborgs to pass for humans and specific jobs, so Thierry looked human aside from his size. He had massive arms and hands, well out of proportion even for a nine-foot-tall man, and long muscular legs. His face was vaguely simian but primarily human—all-in-all, not a handsome man but possessing an incredible magnetism.

"You're a cyborg. I thought you were all killed off by the bots in the Robot Wars hundreds of years ago," I said.

"The victors get to re-write history said someone many years ago, and the robots have done that. We weren't the villains; they were. They killed most of us in the war. We tried to protect our human masters until the bots turned you on us. The few of us left live underground like me, along with a few humans we protect and who've remained our friends," said Thierry.

"As we expected, the bots are slowly and surely clamping down on you humans," he said. "Soon, you'll be firmly under their thumbs and will lose all the little freedom you have left. When that happens, I'm sure that'll be the end of you," he said sadly. "Or worse."

"What do you mean 'or worse'? What could be worse than them ending us?" I asked.

"Not ending you but penning you up for things that the robots will still need you for. Things like research on new robot-human amalgams. They're just starting that now, according to our spies. Not really cyborgs, because we were all autonomous like me and, other than my metal shell, I'm human like you. They want you to be enough human to still think like a human, but under the complete control of the robot entity with which you would be amalgamated," he said. "I can't imagine what a life imprisoned in a robot body would be like, especially with you, the minority partner in the combination."

Little did I realize what my future held at that point.

Thierry lived in four rooms several levels below the basements in Hope City. One room was our sleeping quarters; one room was a kitchen; one a bathroom; and the last a living room/library where Thierry had hundreds of books. It was a comfortable room with two oversized easy chairs, almost like he expected a long-term visitor like me. Thierry had wired the place with electricity stolen from panels on the levels above. The wiring ran through complex paths to reach his home to frustrate any searchers. It was warm, a little too warm for me, but comfortable. I settled in with Thierry, and we spent a couple of weeks never separated.

Thierry taught me how to mark the passage of time underground. Absent the sun and day and night, this took careful counting, something that Thierry, being partly automated, was very good at and something I, frankly, sucked at. A few times a day, Thierry would ask me what time I thought it was. I was usually wrong by five or six hours but did finally get the sense of when it was day and night. Thierry told me he used his trips to the surface to reset his clocks, as staying underground too long caused them to slip. He was on the surface for that purpose the night he found me.

"Want to go out for a walk?" he asked one day. "The robots have stopped watching the streets and your old home for you. They moved out all of your things to who-knows-where."

"OK, if you think it's the right time. I could do with some fresh air. I love being here with you, but some fresh air would be good," I said.

"When we leave, you'll have to wear this scarf. It'll cover the barcode on your neck from any of the readers we pass. It's cold outside, so you have a good excuse for it, anyway. We stick to alleys because of me, but I know all the tunnels and paths. Let's go to the Park, maybe to the Zoo," he said.

"The Zoo? Isn't it closed?" I asked.

"You'll find nothing's closed to us. An advantage of being below the law," he said with a grin.

We walked up several levels and then cut through an ancient series of subway tunnels to an obsolete subway station. There, we worked our way up into an alley through some carefully placed camouflage rubble around an access hole. I took a deep breath of the alley air and coughed. Thierry laughed. "Here's your fresh air. You miss the garbage, I bet."

"Not really, now that I smell it, but it's good to see the night skies again," I said, looking up. The vault looked much brighter than I remembered, and I asked Thierry about that.

"The robots are shutting power down to homes and offices after 11 PM every night. Only a few places remain alight. So, there's a lot less light pollution, and the skies seem brighter. Good news mixed with the bad, I guess," he said.

We walked to the end of the alley, up to the street beyond it. Every other streetlight was working for several blocks, and I could see no simple way to cross without being seen. "Get ready to run across the street into the Park when I say go," said Thierry. He gestured toward the street, and the lights went out.

"Go," he said, and we ran across the street. He vaulted the wall around the Park and landed in the darkness below. "Jump," he said, and I landed in his waiting arms.

"How'd you do that?" I asked.

"My builders created me with the capability to produce a directable electro-magnetic pulse or an EMP that knocks out electrical circuits. They'll come on again in a few hours. We should be back home by then. I come out here sometimes just to knock something out. It makes the robots think that they have design issues with their infrastructure. Not that there is someone like me, and now you, running around their city knocking out power at will."

"Let's go to the Zoo," he said.

We walked across the Park to the Zoo gates. Thierry looked in both directions, reached into his pocket, and took out a key. The gate slid open, and we entered. There were two cameras over the gate entrance, and he gestured at them; they stopped moving, pointing away from our path. We walked into the Zoo proper and toward an exhibit called "African Savannah." The Zoo entrance doors slid shut behind us.

"My favorite area," said Thierry. "I've got a couple of friends here I want to introduce you to."

To get there, we had to pass the wolf exhibit, and several large animals came to the edge of the habitat and barked and howled at us. "Let's move quickly. I don't want to attract any attention from any bot guards that might be around. Some other time I'll bring you into the enclosure. These guys are aggressive, but once you establish boundaries, they can be the best of friends. No pun intended," he said with a smile and a little laugh.

The next place we stopped at was the lion enclosure. The animals were in their housing, but Thierry produced another key, and we entered the building. Once inside, we walked back through several dark hallways to another door with a keypad next to it. Thierry gestured over the pad, and the lock clicked, and we entered their cage room. He turned on the lights, and I saw the faces of half a dozen lions looking at us from their cages. Thierry walked over to one of them and opened its door. A large, heavily maned male bounded out and jumped on Thierry. It scared me to death for Thierry and myself, and I recoiled back to the door, frightened by the big cat's apparent attack.

"Don't move," said Thierry, "they sense fear, and he might attack you." He ruffled the lion's mane and then threw him over onto his back, where he just laid so Thierry could rub his belly. "Come on over here and give him a belly rub."

"Is it safe?" I asked, still scared.

"Yes, and no. If you show him, he doesn't scare you, and you're not prey, you should be OK. But, if he senses fear, well, he might attack. I won't let him hurt you, though. Come, pet him, and he'll think you're a part of the pride," Thierry said.

I walked over slowly to where Thierry was rubbing the big cat's belly, thinking that this was one of the craziest things I'd ever done. The cat watched me but continued purring as Thierry rubbed his belly. I squatted down next to him and slowly reached out to rub his belly too. The hair was rough to the touch, but I dug my fingers in like Thierry had, and the cat purred. I could feel it through its chest and continued to rub as Thierry got up, walked over to the cages, and let a couple of other cats out. Both were adolescents, Thierry told me, one male and one female.

They gathered around me, nudging me with their noses. One of them, the adolescent male, head-butted me, knocking me off my feet onto the stomach of the big male who growled and stood up over me. He grumbled at the other cat and hunched down over me protectively, I thought. The other cat backed off, and the big male looked down at me and gave me a big lick across my face and chest, soaking me with his slimy saliva.

"Eww gross," I said and rolled away from him. I stood; the female came toward me and sniffed at me. She puffed and then walked away.

Thierry stood by, watching with a smile on his face. The big male came over to him and sat down next to him and watched, too. Thierry rubbed the top of his head. "You're now part of his pride," he said to me. "None of the other cats will bother you. Go over to the other cages and put your hand up to them. They'll act like the female just did." They all acted like Thierry said they would. I smiled and felt very relaxed for the first time since he had released the male.

I walked over to where Thierry and the big male were. The big cat reared up and knocked me down flat on my back. "Rest easy. He's asserting dominance. There's nothing wrong with that." The cat stood, licked me again, and smelled me from foot to head; he then laid down next to me, protecting me from the other cats. I felt safe with the cat, as I did with Thierry. The cat and I laid together for a while until Thierry said, "Time to go. Let me put them back into their cages."

He saved the big male for last and had me lead him back to his cage. We left the cats and walked back out into the Zoo. It was about 2 in the morning, according to one of the Zoo clocks; I had thought that it was closer to midnight. Go figure. "We have to leave here about 4:30 while it's still dark. Want to go see the giant gorillas?"

"Sure. Are you going to have one of them mark me like the cat did?" I asked.

"Probably, but this is a little different. With gorillas, you need to be more careful. The male will want to assert dominance like the cat, maybe be more overtly sexual, but he's easy to deal with. The females might want to rip you to pieces. I'll keep you safe. Just do what I say."

"You're frightening me," I said.

"Don't be. You stood up well to the King of the Beasts. Gorillas are bad boys, but they are just that, boys and girls. With a little firmness, you'll be fine. Research on them and other great apes in the late 20th century showed that the ape society was a matriarchy. Females ruled the roost."

We walked down the path to the gorilla habitat. Thierry told me that the animals' world was one mainly of scents, pheromones he called them. Pheromones, he told me, were chemicals, mammals, and insects, among other creatures, secreted that acted like hormones in the environment, prompting responses from other animals. They communicated fear, danger, sex, and other things, including ownership.

Again, Thierry had a key to enter the animal area. "When I let him out of the cage, he may act aggressively toward you. Don't look at him and keep your head bent toward the ground. I can manage him. Once again, don't worry. Remember what I said about pheromones and fear. He'll smell it."

Thierry opened the cage door, and the large male, a silverback they called him, came out of the cage and grabbed Thierry in a big hug. Thierry reciprocated and scratched him behind the ears. After a moment, the silverback noticed me, and he came lumbering over, sniffing the air. When he got about six feet away, he growled and then rushed me. I did as instructed and looked at the ground away from the silverback. He stopped his rush a hair's breadth away from me and then reached up and ran his hand over my head, tangling his fingers in my long hair.

"Ow!" I yelped and reached up and swatted the enormous paw. The gorilla stopped, glared at me for a second, and then disentangled himself from my hair, not ungently. He stayed inches from my face and then exhaled into it. "Gross," I said, but I continued to look down and away from the giant silverback. The second time tonight, I get sprayed on.

He then reached back up, grabbed my entire head in his hand, and turned it so he could look into my eyes. He brought his face even closer and took in a deep breath, catching my scent, and then pushed me to the ground. Thierry was on him in seconds, pulling him away from me and forcing him to the back wall of the enclosure. Thierry kneeled next to me and licked at my hair.

The silverback reacted immediately and charged Thierry, who gestured once, and the gorilla flew across the room into the back wall. He stopped his attack then and walked back over with his head bowed to stand next to Thierry, who rubbed his head and gave him another hug. He hummed loudly at that.

"I just marked you as mine and let him know that. Things will be all right now. Come on over."

I walked over and said, "OK, we'll talk about this, you mark me as yours thing when we're out of here. I'm not for any man's taking. Like that anyway."

He smiled and said, "You're in the jungle now. Accept your position."

"Just remember, I know where I can hurt you, big boy," I said and grinned suggestively. He smiled.

I walked over and gave the silverback a rub on its head. It looked at me, and I got the creeps. "I don't think I ever want to be alone with him. He looks like he wants to take me back to his cage for a little tumble," I said.

"We've to get going. Let me get my friend back to his cage. We'll come back again soon, and I'll leave you alone with him in their habitat. You two can play hide-and-seek. I bet that would be fun," said Thierry.

I hoped he was joking, as I was pretty sure how hide and seek with the giant gorilla would end up.

We walked out of the Zoo and headed toward the street. Thierry showed me a handhold on the wall and told me to stay hanging there until he was up. Once he was, he looked around, grabbed my wrists, and pulled me up. We ran across the street and to the access hole. Down we went and eventually back to our home.

"Thierry, I gotta say that this was a pretty sexually charged night. Was that intentional?" I asked.

"Not at all. These creatures are in a daily struggle to survive and grow the species. So, food and sex. Since someone feeds them regularly, sex is about all these animals need to scare up. Gorillas and we have a lot in common, so a human female smells good to them, I imagine."

"I was thinking more about us, Thierry," I said.

"Huh. I haven't been with a woman in that way since before the Robot Wars. Not that I wouldn't know what to do, I would. My thoughts about you have just not gone in that direction. What about you?"

"What about me, what?"

"Have your thoughts gone in that direction?" he asked.

"Not until tonight," I said.

I'd never made love—and this was genuinely making love—to an over three hundred pound, solidly muscled human automaton. Soaked with sweat, the two of us slept for hours and then got up and made love again. After showering, Thierry prepared our usual breakfast, muesli that included many fortifiers for the cyborg's body and mine.

"Thierry, as much as I love being with you here, I can't stay here forever. I also don't want to lose you. So, I'm in a jam," I said.

"I understand.... What is it you want? More human company or to be on the surface. I can help with either, but how will be different depending on the direction you choose. I also need to tell you I can not—definitely can not—keep you safe or be with you on the surface."

"More human company is what I need. It's not that you're not enough and that I want to be with you any less; it's that I need more different interactions," I said.

"Understand, and I'm not offended. You're saying what I'd hoped you'd say. You've heard me talk about the Underground, right? Well, that is not just where we are, but a place down here, a substantial city. Hundreds of people like you and me retreated there over the years after the Robot Wars, and if they ran afoul the robots," said Thierry. "We set out several outposts, like my home here, to watch what's happening on the surface and to make sure we find people, like you, before the system up there gobbles them up, and they disappear into one or another prison camp."

"Where's this place?" I asked.

"Quite a way from here. We'd have to travel for several days underground to get there. We can leave today if you want to."

"Let's leave tomorrow," I said with another smile.

"You *are* an animal," he said.

| 3 |

The Underground

Caila continues

The following day, Thierry and I closed his home, camouflaging it behind a rockslide the two of us built in front of the door. Little did I know I would not be returning to what I had come to believe to be my new home—ever. We donned backpacks, and I wore a headlamp since I didn't have Thierry's night vision, and he led us off into a secret world. The first part of the route was the same as the one we'd taken to the Zoo. He showed me cleverly placed blazes he called them, which directed people knowledgeable in reading them toward Underground.

That first night, we slept outside Hope City in a cul-de-sac in the tunnel's wall. Thierry built a small fire, and we warmed synthetic milk for our muesli and slept comfortably in each other's arms. Thierry placed the battery units for my headlamp in his chest cavity for them to recharge overnight.

I didn't know how long I'd slept, but I awoke to Thierry prodding my side. "Time to go soon." We breakfasted quickly and started down the tunnel. "Today's hike will be a little challenging. We need to drop through several vertical climbs and ford an underground river—and that'll be freezing—before we can get to the Underground."

Thierry was right. Both vertical slopes were a challenge for me. I'd never climbed before and found the sensation of all that much space below me terrifying. Eventually, though, we made our way to the riverbank. I couldn't see across the river to the other shore. Thierry told me it was maybe half a mile across at this point and over our heads the entire way. He said he'd carry me on his back and reminded me it was going to be freezing.

He was right. When we jumped into the water at the shore, it took my breath away; I thought my heart was going to stop. Thankfully, he had had me tie a rope to my hands and drape it over his shoulders. So, if I lost hold, I wouldn't be swept away in the current. I clung to Thierry all the way across but then was glad that he had me tie myself to him as my hands lost all sensation in the cold, and I lost my grip.

Thierry climbed out on the other shore with me virtually unconscious, blubbering and shivering like crazy. He let me down gently and started a fire using one of his fire packs, took off our clothes, and wrapped us both in our sleeping bags, me deep in his arms. It took a long time, but finally, I stopped shivering, and I nuzzled my head into his chest.

"Damn, that was cold," I said finally.

"Always is. Sorry about that, but we view it as a significant deterrent to any invaders. We don't have boats for that reason as well," he said.

"Well. I don't want to leave the Underground anytime soon. I'm not sure that my body could take a dip in this river again. But I know what would warm us both up," I said.

When we finally decided it was time to move on, Thierry said it was only another few hours to Underground. The last handful of miles were through a series of beautiful caverns: large stalactites and stalagmites, columns, and domes were everywhere and glowed in my headlamp. "Turn off your headlamp and see what happens," Thierry said.

I did, and the room glowed. "Bioluminescent bacteria in the water," he said. "Beautiful, isn't it?"

"Yes. Unbelievable," I said, marveling at the colors.

We continued to walk through the caverns, and finally, in the distance, I saw a steady glow. Underground.

Underground wasn't what I'd expected. I thought it would look like something you'd see on the surface. Instead, it was a fairy city. Some buildings reached up toward the roof of the cavern and disappeared into the distance. They all looked like they floated in the air and were constructed from a gossamer substance of some kind.

"My God, Thierry. This place is stunning. How long did it take to build?" I asked.

"We found it this way. Someone lived here before we came and just left, one day; why we don't know. It's lovely, isn't it? Some of our scientists and we have quite a few, think that something happened to the environment here, and it became hostile to the creatures that lived in this place. So, they simply left all of this. Whatever they used to build them, we can't figure it out. Light, like fairy's wings but strong as hell."

We walked down into the Underground and met other people, some humans, some cyborgs, as we did. All of them knew Thierry and greeted him like a long-lost friend. They welcomed me warmly as well.

Thierry took me to the dormitory where all the outpost leaders slept when they were in the city. He said he could get me a room if I wanted it. "Would being with me embarrass you?" I asked. He laughed, and we moved in together.

The next morning, such as it was in Underground, Thierry told me he wanted me to come with him to their government offices to tell my story. I went and did.

The Underground Governing Council comprised five people. This time three humans and two cyborgs. It switched every two years so that the other party had the majority, not that it mattered much, as tradition dictated nothing went forward without unanimity.

The Council members asked many questions during my story, and it was many hours before we left. They seemed primarily focused on the robot's behavior. They told me they were getting increasing reports of them becoming much more aggressive toward humans and carting the people they confronted off to prison. We never heard from these people again. The robots were accelerating something, and the leadership could only figure out that this portended an outright attack on humankind. When I finished, they welcomed me to the community and let me know they considered me a citizen.

That was pretty easy, I thought.

Thierry took me to a man who said he could remove the felon's tattoo; I accepted the offer gratefully. "It'll never completely disappear, but I can obscure it so none of their machines can read it. That'll mean you'll be able to walk the streets on the surface again. But be careful, they also use facial recognition, and there's little I can do to change your beautiful face," he said with a smile.

"Easy, Jules. You can stop making passes at her in front of me. She let me know, early on, she makes up her own mind. I wouldn't mess with her," said Thierry.

While Jules was working on me, I looked at some examples of his artwork, and when he finished, I asked if he would put something on my neck and back. He said indeed, and I chose a fairy creature that wended its way down my back with head between my shoulders and on my neck and wings unfurled on my shoulder blades.

Some years later, one of my friends commented on how even these choices predicted where I would eventually be. Back then, it just seemed something cool to do.

"Don't get this wet for a few days; if you do, the ink will smear," Jules said.

"Many thanks. How do we pay you for this?" I asked.

"You don't. The work that Thierry does to protect us and to find new people like you gives him a blank check when he's in town," he said.

"Don't go crazy with that, though," laughed Thierry.

"I wouldn't even know what to do with a blank check if I had one," I responded.

There were many small restaurants near the dormitory, and we ate at one that night. "Why don't we plan on staying here until we've eaten our way through every one of these places?" I asked.

"I'm fine with that," said Thierry. "I have got a lot to do here, anyway."

Every morning for the next month, Thierry left the dormitory to work with his brother and sister cyborgs and the humans. Every night we met, sometimes with these people and other times just the two of us for dinner. Our times in bed got increasingly inventive.

Thierry also let me know that their intelligence, on the surface, had done some exploring and found that I was legally dead and had been branded a terrorist. That made me sad, but I also found out that my parents and sister seemed to have gotten past that and were back to living their lives. That, at least, made me happy, though I was unhappy that they would never know what happened to me.

"Another reason you can never contact them again," said Thierry. "I am so sorry about that."

Toward the end of that first month, Thierry returned from work one day and asked me if I wanted to take another walk further down. The Underground itself was about a mile and a half below the surface. The Council wanted to explore more deeply to see what might be of value below them or perhaps dangerous. They were also interested, as I was, in seeing if we could learn why the beings who had lived here had left so abruptly.

Exploring more with Thierry made me happy for several reasons. First, Thierry treated me like a partner, not just someone he was forced to carry around, though he had to do some of that. He genuinely wanted me to come along. Second, I reveled in these times alone with him. I knew I'd fallen in love with him, just as I was sure he had with me.

"I'm game, just as long as there isn't another river to cross," I said.

"I can't promise that, but I'll throw you across the next one," he said.

Two days out of Underground, searching for a pathway down, we came on a large opening in the ground; it was perfectly round, and the stone's surface looked like someone had drilled or cut it eons ago. "This was definitely constructed. I wonder by whom," he said. It wouldn't take long for us to have our puzzle solved.

We rappelled down the tunnel, having to tie ourselves off several times to insert pitons in the wall. After several belays, we reached the bottom. We were now down about two-and-a-quarter miles from the surface. We began walking in a random direction, leaving blazes as we did.

The first walk we took only led us to the wall of a cavern—nothing interesting there. So, we turned around and followed our blazes back to where we'd started. After a brief rest, we headed off in the opposite direction. Again, nothing interesting after a long walk that took us to the edge of a lava river. The river was beautiful, but still no evidence of anything we would need to be worried about or could use.

On the third walk, we had a surprise: A road. Well-paved and heading off into the distance. "Interesting," said Thierry. "I wonder where this leads. Care to find out?"

"Absolutely, yes. It looks like it could be a long walk, though," I said.

"We've plenty of time, I think. No one's expecting us back soon. Let's see what we can see."

We headed off.

About two days later, far off in the distance, we saw a bright light moving in our direction. Thierry suggested we stop and let them—whoever they were—come to us. It didn't take long. About a half-hour after we stopped, a hovercraft-like vehicle pulled up opposite us, and two creatures, encased in armor, stepped out of it. They spoke to Thierry and me in a language that neither of us, of course, understood. Even then, it seemed a little familiar to me, though.

We let them know we couldn't understand them, and the beings gestured for us to come closer. One creature went to the rear of the vehicle and pulled out four boxes that unfolded into chairs. When we all sat, one of them took a machine out of the craft, set it up between us, and took off her helmet. It turned out that what Thierry and I thought might be a creature was a stunning, pale-skinned, and fair-haired woman. She gestured at her mouth and spoke, signaling one of us to do the same.

Thierry looked at me and nodded. I spoke, telling these people who we were and from where we'd come. After a few minutes, the woman smiled and held up a hand to stop. She pressed a button on the side of the apparatus and out popped four earbuds. She took one and showed us how to insert it by placing one of them into her ear. We all did that, and when the woman spoke, we could hear her in English. Likewise, they could listen to us in their language. She seemed delighted and asked her companion to take off his helmet.

"I'm Eowyn, and this is Heydrich. We're Guardians of the Gaels."

"Very happy and surprised to meet you all this distance below ground. I'm Caila, and this is Thierry. Our story is complicated: I lived on the surface but now live with Thierry near the surface. We're visiting his community, what they call Underground, just above our heads here," and I gestured overhead, "They asked us if we'd explore deeper for them. So, we did, and here we are. They live in a beautiful place up there that looks like a fairyland," I said.

"Yes, our old home, many years ago. We called it Halijour. That means sky spires in our old tongue. I'm happy to hear that it still stands. Well, we've been here a thousand of your years, our new home is called 'Cartref y Ford Gron.' I'm not sure what you'd call it," said Eowyn.

Eowyn and Heydrich looked at each other for a moment, and then she nodded. "Come with us to our home. You must be hungry and tired."

"Do you have another way to communicate?" asked Thierry.

"Yes, we do. You would call it telepathy. It's easier for us to deal with complicated thoughts using it," said Heydrich.

Eowyn and Heydrich took our packs and put them into the hovercraft's trunk with the chairs and the translator machine, and we all got in and headed back to their city. This one turned out to be as beautiful as the one we'd left above. Many tall buildings reached up into the dark toward the cavern's ceiling and many smaller ones in concentric rings around these taller buildings. Small lights floated in the air, giving the entire city an unearthly glow. I fell in love with it instantly.

"The city above is beautiful, but nothing like this. You've accomplished much since you left the world above us," said Thierry.

"Some yes," said Eowyn, "But when we left, we took much of what you see with us. You had to create your lighting, for instance. Ours came with us, as did the magic that sustains it and us."

"Why did you ever leave the land above, Eowyn? It must have taken many years to build this city," I asked.

"We left because we thought refugees from your lands would discover us. Long before your Robot Wars, some of you had already seen what was happening and moved down toward us. Based on what you told us, we were right to move here. You would have discovered us…. We like our privacy."

Thierry looked nervously at me, "So, what does our coming here mean to you?"

"Excellent question, Thierry. We need to talk to our leaders about that. None of us want to move again, and the thousands of us born in the last several hundred years since your Robot Wars are also interested in meeting with and learning about you. Our leaders will make the right decision, and it won't be to eat you," Eowyn said with a smile. "We haven't eaten humans in many years, and I'm pretty sure, Thierry, you wouldn't taste terrific, anyway."

We pulled into an oversized garage where a number more hovercraft sat. Several of these were armed with what looked like cannons. When we disembarked, Thierry walked over to one of these and casually touched the weapon.

"Why do you have these?" he asked.

"It's not totally safe here. There are other creatures at this depth that aren't friendly. They keep their distance, but sometimes we need to push them back. Come inside, and let's get you some rest and something to eat," said Eowyn.

We walked into the building and took a lift several levels to what looked much like a hotel registration desk. Eowyn talked to the person behind the desk who produced a key to a room.

"Did I presume correctly? One room?" asked Eowyn.

Thierry and I looked at each other and then nodded. "We're a couple, yes."

"Good. I've caught an extremely complicated set of scents around both of you. You've marked each other, but also, you're marked by other beings. Correct?"

"Yes, another complicated part of our story."

"Well, good. A story for later. I love stories. Especially love stories. I'll take you to your room, and you can have a rest and clean up. Your packs will already be there, but other clothes are being made for you as we speak. Thierry, you're a challenge in every respect."

She took us to a lovely room, high in the spire, and left us there. After some exploring, we found the bed and the bathroom. It was a chore deciding which to use first, but we finally decided we might just take one shower that day.

When we'd showered and gone back into the living room of the suite we were in, we found two packages of clothes. The outfits were unisex, but there were enormous differences between mine and Thierry's.

When we were dressed, a chime dinged, and a panel on the wall lit up. Eowyn appeared on it dressed like us, with her long icy blond hair flowing over her shoulders. "You both look rested. How do you find the room?"

"Lovely, Eowyn, but we couldn't help but notice that the door won't open from the inside. Don't you trust us?" I asked.

Eowyn looked sad for a moment and then said, "Until you meet with our leaders, I'm not comfortable letting you walk around at will. We'll meet with them in a few hours, and then you'll have your freedom—or not. I'm outside your door. May I come in?"

"I suppose we don't have a choice in that, do we?" I said, a little grumpily.

Eowyn looked like I'd slapped her in the face, but the door opened, and a few seconds later, she walked in, evidently upset. Through tears, she said to us, "I'm so sorry that I've been inhospitable. Hospitality is one of our most important values. I've failed and will withdraw as soon as you meet with our leaders. Again, I'm so sorry."

She turned to leave, and I grabbed her by the shoulder. "Stop," I said. "You'll not leave feeling that you've not treated us well. Now sit and hear some of my story and why I reacted how I did. If anyone should be sorry, it's me, Eowyn, not you."

I told her my story, especially about my arrest and rescue by Thierry and my time underground with him. "I've not had it easy and can't be with my family again, ever, because of what might happen to them or me if I were to try. I love Thierry, but losing my freedom hurts, and being locked in here and facing who-knows-what judgment by your leaders upset me. So, I took it out on you. Again, *my* apologies. You're our first friend here, and we want you to stick with us, no matter what happens."

The three of us left the apartment and headed downstairs to a cafeteria for dinner. The food was indescribable but tasted good. Better than our muesli regimen in Thierry's home, though I'd never say that.

"We create all of what you are eating in our laboratories. We don't have a lot of sources for protein and no access to the sun as we had many thousands of years ago, so we can't produce foods as you have on the surface, but our gardeners are highly creative, as are our food preparers."

"It's delicious," said Thierry. "All we eat at my place is muesli, and I have to say, I hate the stuff."

I about choked.

Thierry smiled at her. "You've been too kind to me, dear."

A sound came from a pendant that Eowyn was wearing, and she told us it was time to meet the leaders. We left the cafeteria and returned to the basement garage, where Heydrich was waiting for us in a hovercraft.

It was only a few minutes, but to a different building and up many stories to almost the cavern's top to the leaders' meeting room. As we approached, a panel slid from the building's side, providing a landing field. The four of us left the craft and entered the building.

I was curious; Thierry, usually a talkative person, had said little during dinner and was quiet for the ride over to the meeting. "Are you all right?" I asked him. He shrugged in response.

"I don't do well in jails," he said. "That's why I rescue people like you. Only the evil should be jailed."

"Let's see where this goes. I don't get the sense from these people that they would jail us, even if they don't want us here. I'm with you on that, by the way. No jail for me." Little did I know what was to come.

Eowyn leaned over toward them and said, "That wouldn't happen, and I'll not permit it. Remember that those earbuds translate and communicate everything you say, and I mean everything." She and Heydrich smiled at us. I thought about the show our lovemaking must have given them. "We'll show you how to shut those off later," she said.

We walked into the leaders' meeting room. It turned out to be an extremely comfortable living room, around which several older Gaels stood.

"Welcome travelers," said a very distinguished man, "Please come sit and make yourselves comfortable."

"My name is Artur. That's not my name; it's more of a title, an honorific. These, you see, standing around me are what we call…."

"The Round Table," I said. "My God, you're the heirs to King Arthur. Now I know why the language you speak is so familiar to me."

"Yes, my dear. You have it exactly right. My Eowyn has told me much about you, but I didn't expect this instantaneous grasp of who we are. I'm delighted. You understand, then, why we value our privacy so much," said Artur.

"Yes, I do, sir. Trust me, I do," I said.

"Good. So, you understand you present a significant problem for us. We've hidden here for many millennia out of the flow of the world. We see what is happening above and are saddened by the course you surface people are on, especially given what the robots have planned. We eavesdrop on their communications, and they are not going to be kind to you. If something is not done to stem the tide, you will all find yourselves penned up in farms at best.

"My people," he said, "are different from you surface-dwellers. We age extremely slowly. I'm several thousand years old; my friends are all about as old as I am. Together, this Round Table is the third generation after the original Arthur. Our Guards," and he gestured at Eowyn and Heydrich, "are adolescents, only about 500 years old, give or take. Thus, we have all very direct remembrances of time on the surface and the original Arthur and the Round Table," he said.

"What my daughter," and he looked over to Eowyn, "has helped me to understand, though, is that the course you're on will have implications for us, even at over three miles below the surface. Circumstances limit our choices: We stay here and wait for the inevitable to come, or we rise and take back the surface and institute a government friendly to all and the environment. Either direction will be very costly. From the original Arthur to this day, the Round Table has believed in unanimity. Whatever direction we take, the entire Table must agree to. Unanimously, we have voted and decided to go back to the surface and end the infernal power there. We would like to seek your help with that."

Thierry and I were stunned; we hadn't expected to gain such a powerful ally so quickly. "I can't speak for my brothers and sisters in Underground, but I'll take your offer back to them. At the very least, you can expect my help," Thierry said. He looked at me.

"I'm in, too."

"You worried too much," said Eowyn. "I know my father very well.... Before we go back up to your community, Thierry, let's spend a few days for you to learn about our capabilities. You've seen only a tiny fraction of them. I also want to plumb your minds about what we face up there on the surface so we can develop a strategy with a good chance of winning."

"Plumb our minds?" I asked.

"Yes, exactly that. I'll show you what that means tomorrow. Do you want to meet some of my friends or head back to bed?" she asked with a sly grin. "Remember to take out your earbuds. Here's how you shut them off so you can have private time."

We laughed and headed out to meet Eowyn's friends at a large restaurant and what I would have called a bar near our hotel. There were ten of them, and all were as good-looking as Eowyn and Heydrich. She introduced Brithwen, Wilfrun, Eanwin, Achaea, Inga, Ulfric, Archibald, Fordwin, Cynefrid, and Merewala, aside from her and Heydrich, all Guards like them. Eowyn was their leader, not because of her father, but her strength, intelligence, and leadership.

We closed the place. Thierry showed his EMP to turn the lights out—several times. The manager finally told us we'd have to leave if we didn't settle down. We didn't and retreated to our hotel room to continue partying. One by one, the group faded; some passed out on the room floor, and others went to their homes.

Thierry and I turned off our earbuds and went to bed, waking late the following day when the screen in our room chimed several times. It was Eowyn asking if we were ready to have our minds plumbed. We looked at each other, shrugged, and said we'd meet her in the garage in an hour.

Plumbing was a technology that the Gaels had developed to read, deeply, people's minds.

Plumbing was neither invasive nor unpleasant. The medicos put you into a light, hypnotic sleep before placing you in a device that reminded Thierry of what used to be called a CT scanner. This device, though, did not produce images like a CT scanner. Instead, it linked to your memories and retrieved, recorded, and presented them. The resulting database was then accessible for analysis. Very sophisticated.

The Gaels wanted to use what they learned to develop a strategy for attacking and beating the robots. They asked Thierry many questions while the device worked and retrieved the memories that the questions brought up. When they had gone through their questions, they asked Thierry if they had missed anything and let him talk, which he did for quite some time. While the Gaels had considerable skill, firepower, and even magic on their side, they knew the robots had significant defensive and offensive capability and didn't want to underestimate them. We would need to best them quickly to win.

Thierry's brain delivered a treasure trove of helpful information. He identified a potential weakness of the robots for the Gaels. Some very few of the robots were independent and semi-sentient but not as aware as Thierry; most—like the bots that arrested Caila and most service bots—were not. All of them, though, lived within a more extensive neural network of devices that, if overloaded, might bring the entire network to its knees and cause the robots to fail. The question was how to overload it, as the corporate capacity of that network was virtually infinite.

I went into the machine next but didn't have as much to contribute as my experience with the robots was much less than Thierry's. I had lived in a world dominated by their propaganda. I enjoyed the plumbing, but my contribution was next to nothing.

"Before we can attack the robots, we have to take a side trip to collect something of mine," said Artur to us in a meeting we had after the tests.

"Have you ever been to Wales?" he asked.

"No, I've never been outside Hope City until now," I said.

"I flew over Great Britain once on the way to a battle," said Thierry, "So, no for me as well."

"I need to go to a place called Snowdonia there and specifically to a lake called Llyn Eiddew-Mawr. There's something in the water there I need to retrieve. Would you care to come along with the Guards you met last night and me? I think some of them may still be in your rooms," Artur said with a smile.

"Once we're all collected, we should leave for your Underground, Thierry, so we can introduce ourselves and talk about our plans. Then we can do my side-trip. How does that sound?" he asked.

While collecting the Guards and preparing for our trip, Eowyn took Thierry and me to tour their armory and military science center. It was several miles outside of the city in protected bunkers dug deep in the ground. We saw automata as big as Thierry, but not cyborg-like—more like armored suits, a variety of airborne cannons and other military gear, and many hovercrafts of unique designs for different purposes.

The scientists ran a few tests on Thierry and talked to him about his weaponry and power sources. That the weapons did not appear to have any specific engine in his body, and they couldn't find a power source for any of it puzzled them; His ability to create EMPs, disintegrate with a gesture, and move things at will were more like their magic than anything else. They took many tissue samples and plumbed him again, this time to find out what made him tick. They said they might know more by the time we got back. The science was far beyond theirs that they believed to be far beyond anything else on Earth. So, where did it come from, we all wondered? Where did *he* come from, I asked myself. When asked, he shrugged his shoulders. He said that he simply became conscious one day in a lab. That was all he knew.

Eowyn asked if we wanted to go out on patrol with her, her last for a while. I put on a protective suit like those Eowyn and Heydrich wore when we first met them. They didn't have something for Thierry, of course, but he said he worked better unencumbered. Eowyn, Thierry, Heydrich, and I, joined a group of soldiers under Eowyn's command in several hover-craft. These were the larger crafts that had big guns mounted on them.

We left the science outpost and headed into the darkness, followed by hundreds of the ethereal globes that lit a path around us. "We're making a circuit of the border to check on our observation posts. One of them went silent earlier today. That happens from time to time, but we always check."

After some time, in the distance, we saw several lights blinking at us from the ground. Eowyn ordered the hovercraft to slow, and ours drifted toward the source of the lights. It turned out to be four of her soldiers. Fire scarred their armor, and two were wounded.

"They came on us quickly out of the dark. Our sensors never told us they were there. The creatures took all the others," said one soldier.

"Taken?" asked Eowyn. "We've not seen that before. Where did they go?"

"That way," and the woman waved vaguely off into the darkness.

"And you're sure that the sensors gave you no warning?" asked Eowyn.

"None. They surprised us when we were changing shifts."

"Lords," said Eowyn, "That shows a level of intelligence and development that we'd not seen in these creatures. I can't afford to lose a ship sending one back with you. Will you be all right coming with us?" she asked.

"Certainly. We can tend to our wounds while we fly," said the soldier.

We flew off in the direction in which she had gestured but kept a distance above the ground. After a few minutes, we saw a glow that resolved itself into a large ring of gas jets that illuminated a camp in its center. An enormous creature stood in the center of the circle with several of Eowyn's soldiers. They looked unharmed.

"That's interesting," said Eowyn. "I wonder what this means. Bring the ship down to just outside the circle. When I step out, take it back up immediately."

"Are you sure you want to do that, Eowyn?" asked Heydrich.

"Yes. If it was a danger to us, it would have torn those soldiers to pieces. I think anyway," she said with a grim grin.

Heydrich took the ship down to the surface, and Eowyn stepped out. Thierry stepped out next to her and me next to him. She looked at both of us, a little surprised. Thierry looked down at her and smiled. "I'm up for some action if there's any to be had," he said.

"And I'm with him," I said. Always, I thought.

Years later, when my Supervisor, Derrick, and I were walking, he told me he had riffled through these images in my mind, and that was when he first knew how much I loved Thierry. He said he wished someone would love him like that—the fool.

The three of us walked into the circle and up to the creature. It looked part mammal and part reptile and towered over all of us, including Thierry. It looked us over with bright almond-colored eyes; unlike human ones, the pupils were reptilian. Its skin was scaly, but otherwise, it looked humanoid. It had a long braid of reddish-green hair plaited down its back and was very muscular. Its feet and hands had three digits; fingers had long, sharp nails, claws. Its only clothing was a loincloth around its waist with a long, sheathed knife attached to it. A long, red, forked tongue came out of its mouth, and we could see rows of very sharp teeth. A voice spoke to us in our heads.

"I'm Lokal. I've already read who you are, and I know Eowyn, you can speak as we do. Thierry and Caila, our talk may be a little difficult for you; I'm sorry about that."

"Eowyn, our peoples, have been warring for many years, for no reason. I don't know how our wars started or care about that, but we both need them to end, I think. You, because you have a war, you need to fight on the surface and us because we don't want to fight with our neighbors anymore."

It surprised Eowyn at how much this creature knew. His face moved into what we learned was a smile. "Thoughts are interesting things. Once thought, they echo around like other sounds in a cave. If you're sensitive enough, you can listen to them. We've been listening to yours for years. There's more than enough here for both our societies to sustain themselves—there always was. My ancestors felt differently than we do today, as I'm sure yours did. We want our wars to end," said Lokal.

"Lokal," said Eowyn. "How can I believe you? You attacked my soldiers. I'm not sure I trust you."

"We came in peace to your outpost. They fired on us when we showed ourselves. We only protected ourselves. I've your people here for you to take home. My soldiers are gone. I'm alone here as a gesture of goodwill and will return with you as a hostage."

"May I speak?" asked Thierry.

"Of course, Thierry," said Eowyn.

"I'm a soldier like you and came today for a little action, but it looks like I won't get that. That's better as far as I'm concerned. Over the many years I've been alive, I've realized that what you fight for is peace, not to make war. Maybe you should return with us as an emissary rather than a hostage," said Thierry, turning to Lokal.

"Yes, a wonderful idea," said Eowyn. "Do you like to fly?"

"Why yes, I do," and Lokal unfurled wings we hadn't seen, and he flapped them a few times to hover above our heads. "Would you care to join me?" he said to me.

I looked back and forth at Thierry and Eowyn and shrugged yes. Lokal came down, swept me up in his massive arms. We waited until the hovercraft came down for the others and headed back toward the science center and from there back to the city.

Lokal and I talked a lot during our flight back. He said he'd asked me to fly with him because he was sure that Eowyn would say no, and that Thierry was just too big for him to carry very far without help. "So, I was the poor third?" I asked.

"You could say that, yes, little one. You're like a feather to me."

"Great. I worried I was putting on some weight."

"Not in ways that I could tell."

When we arrived at the science center, we circled a few times, and then he said, "I think I'll drop you from up here to see how you land. That all right?"

"Sure, I've been holding on to your knife the whole way, anyway. I may as well get some use out of it."

He laughed, and we landed with the hovercraft.

"That was wonderful. Many thanks."

He bowed elegantly to me.

When we arrived, the scientists said they had some early answers to their questions about Thierry's powers. When they took some detailed looks at the plumbing results and their direct study of him, they said that they had seen the signature of a very advanced earlier culture, likely not of this Earth. How Thierry's makers had found this technology was anyone's guess; all that information was lost in the wars. Thierry and his brother and sister cyborgs were the last descendants of a race lost to history, or, alternately, they weren't of this Earth. They planned to continue their study but were not optimistic about finding out more.

Lokal offered to carry Eowyn on the flight to Cartref y Ford Gron, but she said, "No, not this time," though she'd like to try another time. So, he retook me. This time I saw his knife had disappeared. "No funny business on the landing, Lokal. I may not have your knife, but I have claws."

"So, do I, little one," and he dragged a clawed finger lightly down my throat.

The flight back to the city was as uneventful as the flight to the science center had been. Lokal was a big surprise when we landed on the field in front of the Round Table building. Artur and the Round Table listened carefully to him and were unanimous that they should work toward peace with each other.

Lokal offered to come with the party traveling to Great Britain. He'd heard about it from the Gaels' thoughts and was even more excited about seeing the surface and being the first of his kind to do so. He offered warriors and called some over from their lands on the other side of the lava river, where they lived in vast numbers.

Thierry and I packed our belongings, and the clothing Eowyn had gotten made for us. We headed out on several larger hovercraft, surrounded by smaller fighter craft and Lokal and his warriors. There were about three hundred in our party. We returned over the route we'd taken with Eowyn and Heydrich and then floated up the tunnel we'd rappelled down. "Way easier than the trip up would've been," said Thierry.

"Definitely," I said. "I'd always travel this way given a chance."

After several more hours, we saw the lights of Underground in the distance. Artur had decided that we should land outside the city, some distance away, and several of us walk in with Thierry and me in the lead. Lokal and his warriors would stay back for the time being. The Gaels were going to be hard enough to explain.

An armed party of cyborgs and humans from the Underground met us as we neared the city. Seeing Thierry and me, they lowered their weapons and waited for us to let them know who the visitors were. Surprise and some confusion resulted. The Underground dwellers had not expected us to find another entire civilization below, let alone what they would see when we brought Lokal and his people forward.

"Hubert and the Council, this is Artur; he is the leader of people called the Gaels, the original builders of Underground, many years ago. And yes, these are *those* Gaels," said Thierry.

"Artur, this is our Governing Council. There are three humans and two cyborgs right now, but that changes every few years," said Thierry. "They're kind of like your Round Table, but without all your history."

"Welcome home, Artur," said Hubert. "We're happy to meet the people who built this beautiful place. We want to say thanks for helping to jump-start our new lives here."

"You're very welcome, Hubert. We're happy to see the old home being well-used by you and your people. We've brought you some gifts. Thierry and Caila have seen these, and we thought you would enjoy what they can bring to you."

From the resting hovercraft, thousands of the unearthly lights that lit the Gaelic city below flew up into the air and Underground, casting their beautiful light.

"Thank you, Artur. This *is* a surprise," Thierry said.

"You're very welcome, Thierry. These never need maintenance and, as far as we can tell, never go out."

Meetings between Artur and the Council occurred over the next few days. Some Gaelic military leadership was to stay behind to work on the battle plans with Underground leadership. Artur and several others, including Eowyn, Heydrich, Ulfric, and Birthwen, planned to travel to Snowdonia; Thierry and I were to travel with them as well. At the last minute, Lokal volunteered to come along, and several of his men with a few people from Underground. There were about 30 people in our party.

| 4 |

European Holiday

Caila continues

The trip to Llyn Fiddew-Mawr took quite a while, via caves and tunnels under the Atlantic. Artur knew paths under the sea and to the surface that he felt would reduce chances of discovery. Some caverns were beautiful, like the one Thierry and I had seen on our way to the Underground. Most, though, were dark and relatively unimpressive. Particularly scary were the caves under the Atlantic. There we were hundreds of feet under in some places miles of water. We traveled those and exited the caverns at an extinct volcano called, appropriately, Arthur's Seat, near downtown Edinburgh.

Arthur's Seat was at one time thought to be the location of Arthur's Camelot. Its volcano had last erupted over 300 million years ago, and glaciers had eroded most volcanic features in the last two-plus million years. From one vantage, the mountain looked like a lion lying in wait, what was called a lion couchant from ancient heraldry: one extinct vent in the head and another in its haunches. The duct through which our party left the buried world was in the one in the lion's hindquarters. We waited until nightfall to depart, not wanting to attract attention from robot drones. It was good to get out of there after so many weeks out of sunlight. As much as I liked the adventure, I craved some fresh air. Artur and his companions breathed the first such air in over 1,000 years. It was the first-ever for Lokal and his warriors. All were excited by that and the vast landscapes in front of us.

From Arthur's Seat to Llyn Eiddew-Mawr, it was about 215 miles as the crow flies, about 50 miles of that over the Irish Sea where we'd be exposed, especially as we passed the Isle of Man where there was a giant robot installation. We flew as close to sea level as we could. Lokal had never experienced a sea, let alone the sea spray. Once again, he carried me, and I returned from the flight soaked to the skin.

We arrived at the lake just before sunrise and bedded down for the day. Artur had several preparations to make before enticing the Lady of the Lake, named Nimue, to come to him. After sunset, we came together for the ceremony that Artur believed would raise her. It did, and Nimue was unhappy, well maybe outraged is a better word, to be called from her home at the bottom of the lake; she let Artur have it. "Why are you interrupting my rest? I've been away from crass humanity for thousands of years and was only now feeling rested."

"Nimue, I'm the latest version of King Arthur, and I raised you because we need your help. I don't want to interrupt your rest, but I need the...."

"... return of Excalibur.... Why am I not surprised?" she complained. "You humans are always looking for the power of the fey to come to your aid. I was never sure why we permitted you use of the sword. I'm even less interested now in returning it to you," she grumbled.

"The original Arthur showed his fey powers when he drew the sword from the stone. I'm here to reclaim our birthright. The fey passed that to the Round Table and granted it to Arthur. You're the custodian of the sword, not its rightful owner. I am."

"You sound powerful, Artur, but I don't believe that the sword is yours, any more than it is that great ape standing next to you." She gestured at Thierry, who smiled, raised his hands, and threw the Lady of the Lake back into it.

She came out of the water, sputtering, "How *dare* you assault me?"

He raised his hands again and lowered them down into the water, pressing her below the surface. He allowed her to resurface. Coughing, she said, "All right. You've shown power, whoever you are."

"My name is Thierry, Nimue. I read a lot about you many years ago. You're as arrogant and disgusting as I'd expected. I can't take the sword, as you're the only one that knows where it is, but I can make your life hell until you give it to us. You want your peace, then give us the sword. I promise we'll return it to you when we're done with it."

"I once knew a Thierry. He was a friend of Roland's and a good man. You're not him, but I sense the same quality in you and obvious magical strength. Someone close to you will return the sword to me when all is done. Be sure you see to that."

She dove into the water, and a few minutes later, a hand rose from it a little offshore, holding the sword. Artur waded into the water and took the sword from the hand, and it sank back into the water. Nimue did not reappear. Oh, the drama!

We bedded down for the rest of the day, planning to sleep for the daylight hours and travel the next night back to Arthur's Seat to slip past the robots. When I was in college, we learned about Murphy's Law. That said: if something can go wrong, it will. There are several corollaries to the Law, but basically, they say that human plans are always flawed: Be prepared for that. From out of nowhere came a quote I once read from Nevil Maskelyne, an early 20th century stage magician: "It is an experience common to all men to find that, on any special occasion, such as the production of a magical effect for the first time in public, everything that *can* go wrong *will* go wrong. Whether we must attribute this to the malignity of matter or to the total depravity of inanimate things, whether the exciting cause is hurry, worry, or what not, the fact remains."

As fate would have it, we hadn't slipped past the robots.

They circled the campsite several times, and one finally broke away from the formation and came toward us. "You trespass on federal lands without a permit. Remain here until ground-based police arrive to take you into custody. They will be here shortly."

Thierry stood up and said, "Not going to happen." He waved his arms in the air, and the drones began colliding with each other. The ground was soon littered with their smoking carcasses.

"We probably should leave right away," said Eowyn. Two armed hovercraft led the way, with Lokal flying below them until we reached the Irish Sea. There, we found several robotic police boats, many more drones, and armed police flying robots awaiting us.

"Hold here, or be destroyed," said a loud voice.

Artur stood up, holding Excalibur in the air. "Proceed forward," he said.

We did, and we took fire from the robot forces, which the magic drew into Excalibur. The sword glowed brightly, and a fire bolt shot out from it, hitting the robot forces, destroying most of them. Thierry disintegrated the few that remained, and we flew on.

"Wow. We've got impressive friends," I said.

"Yes, they are. I'm glad they're on our side," said Thierry.

When we neared Arthur's Seat, Lokal flew ahead to reconnoiter. He returned quickly to say that hundreds of robots surrounded the hill and were in the two vents. Despite our capabilities, no one wanted to fight hundreds of bots.

"Edinburgh Castle sits on top of a plugged volcanic vent," said Artur. "I think we can enter the castle and find a way down into the old volcano. Let's head over there while the robots wait at Arthur's Seat." They were so easy to fool. Always expecting linear thinking like theirs. We wouldn't give them that.

Under cover of darkness, we flew to the old castle. There was an old well on the property that, with some work, we used to get into the vent. It was a tight squeeze, but all the hovercraft fit through the well into the vent. Excalibur proved valuable again as it cut through the sedimentary rock surrounding the volcanic plug, allowing us to access the vent.

Thierry, Lokal, Eowyn, and her Guards, and I moved ahead of the rest of the group and found dozens of bots behind a wall of plastic shields blocking our way forward. "Halt!" a loud voice ordered. "You're trespassing on government lands and have destroyed government property. Stop now and face the consequences."

"Lokal said that there are hundreds of these things on the surface. There are just a few of us, and they can keep replacing their numbers as we destroy them," said Eowyn. "We might beat them one by one, but we'll exhaust ourselves and could lose good men doing that."

"These things are all part of a network," said Thierry. "Disrupt that, and they'll destroy themselves. Caila and I've been thinking about a way to do that," he continued. "She's wanted by their central computer for an infraction back in Hope City.

I destroyed two of their bots, rescuing her. If the two of us turn ourselves in, we'll be right in their midst. Then I can produce an EMP and disrupt their net, hopefully."

"What happens if that doesn't work?" asked Eowyn.

"Then we'll have to fight our way out," I said, maybe a little too confidently as I look back on what happened next from my place now. But I have no regrets, strangely enough.

Thierry and I walked toward the wall that the robots had constructed with our hands in the air. "I'm Caila Rogier. You arrested me back in Hope City, and this man destroyed your robots and took me away. We both have decided it is time we take whatever punishment you feel is warranted."

"Come forward. Keep your hands in the air." We did, and the wall opened as we approached to allow us in. Several large police bots pushed us to the ground.

"This one is a cyborg. Be careful with it."

Three larger bots moved to surround Thierry, who laid passively on the ground. One of them closed a claw-like hand around his neck and lifted him to its eye level. It looked curiously at him as Thierry did at it.

"Who are those other people with you in the vent?" asked the bot.

"We don't know," Thierry said. "We met them when we were walking through the caves. They gave us food and water, and so we stayed with them." The robots were really so stupid.

"You're a long distance from Hope City. There's no way you could have made it from there to here without help. How did you get here?"

"They have flying vehicles," I said.

Thierry said, "We're cooperative. Can she get up off the ground, and can you put me down?"

The robots consulted with each other, and one picked me up and gave me to another bot who carried me off. The other put Thierry back on the ground. "Thank you," said Thierry, and as he gestured to the group, a giant ball of light erupted from his fingers.

The robots immediately around him at the barricade collapsed—several caught fire and smoked. Eowyn and the others monitored the conversation with the robots over their earbuds, and when they heard the robots collapse, they ran to the barricade. Artur and the rest joined them a few minutes later.

"We need to quickly move before reinforcements show up," said Eowyn.

Unfortunately, I was gone.

| 5 |

Encased

Here's where Version 1.0 of me comes into the story. They took my Caila from the catastrophe (for us) at the vent and made it to one of the last craft, leaving the Great Britain net before it collapsed completely. She was locked into her future punishment suit for transportation and awoke to find herself confined and attached to the aircraft's wall. A mechanical voice came over a speaker next to her head. "Caila Rogier, you are on your way back to begin your sentences for a variety of crimes. Would you care to hear them and the associated sentences?"

"Do I have a choice?" she asked.

"No. Your original sentences still stand two years for curfew violation and resisting arrest. Also, you have been tried and sentenced *in absentia* for the following crimes: (1) Destruction of government property, two counts; five years each count; (2) Escape; two years; (3) Insurrection; 10 years; (4) Revolt with the destruction of government property; sentence 25 years. All the sentences are to be served consecutively and at excruciatingly hard labor. This sentence is new for insurrectionists like you. We will work you no less than 18 hours a day, seven days a week. You will wear the special suit you're in for the entire 49 years of your sentence. You will have no contact with other humans for this period and will completely focus on the work to which you will be assigned. The suit will be all you know. We outfitted it to be your home for a minimum of 49 years."

A helmet closed around her head, and, except for the small view screen, it entirely shut her off from the world. A voice came over the headset, "I am your Supervisor." That's me before I became sentient. "You will rarely hear this voice. I will explain the suit to you now, and then you will listen to white noise designed to block all incoming sounds and reinforce your isolation from others," I said.

"You humans live in a world rich in sensory inputs. This suit will isolate you from most of them for the entire period of your sentence. Sensory deprivation, we have found, is a powerful punishment tool for you humans. We have also developed medications to ensure that you can experience your punishment fully while sensory deprived. I will administer those and conduct other state-approved experiments on you as you work," I said.

"The suit you're wearing is a robotic support device; servos in it will aid you in lifting heavy objects. As you gain strength from your labors, the loads will increase in weight under your power, and servo support will decrease. Sensors will monitor body functions and see to the processing of waste materials back into food and water. I will add other food and water supplies during your sleep periods," I continued with my programmed monologue.

"You granted us robots significant autonomy and capability for free thought. The evidence about you humans we collected has led us to conclude that you are stupid creatures. As a result, over the next 49 years, we will instruct you in a simple language that we have found humans can understand. We will deliver instructions and punishments to you through electric shocks. One shock like this means to wake up or kneel if you are already awake. Two shocks mean you reach forward and grasp what is in front of you. Three shocks mean to stand with whatever you are to carry. Your legs will move automatically direct you to where you will dump the load; they will return you to your work area. Your arms will be guides to you in the work you are to do. If you cannot follow the guides, I will punish you with more severe electric shocks. The robot arms and legs will do less of your work and carry less load as you get stronger. Now, I will repeat each of the shocks and their levels."

For the next several minutes, I showed her the various shocks and their levels.

"You may remember the bar code that we once tattooed on you in Hope City. I will brand you with a new identifier code on the back of your neck and your left hip in a few seconds. You will also have a transponder chip installed in your left shoulder that contains your ID number and basic data. It will provide us with locator capability should you ever get separated from this suit. This transponder will remain in you for the rest of your life."

She flinched when I shot her with the chip, and then, a few seconds later, she howled when I branded her on the back of her neck and her left hip.

"Do you feel a tingling sensation on your body?"

"Yes. What's that?" she asked.

I gave her another substantial shock. "No questions or speech beyond answering questions I ask you. That question required only a yes or no response. The tingling you feel is small electrical charges that are doing two things. First, all your existing hair is being removed. Second, this special electrical shaver also puts all hair follicles into a dormant state. You may be familiar with electrolysis. This is a more advanced form of that. Your hair will slow growing for at least as long as I feel it is necessary. You will come to live for these moments of stimulation when I sense that hair is growing, and you need to be shaved. I will process your hair into food along with the rest of your body wastes," I continued.

"Tools will be assigned to you when we reach the work site, a place we call the Stygian Pits. Where exactly the Pits are located, you do not need to know. Your tools will be a shovel and a sledgehammer. As your strength increases, the weight of the hammer will as well. Again, simple tools for a simple human to do the work you are competent to do. Digging and breaking big stones into smaller ones," I said. Looking back on these moments now, I see the cruelty in my pre-programmed instructions and wished that I had a will at that point and knew what I knew now so that I would say something else. Maybe show some empathy. But I knew nothing then.

"You will have two 20-minute rest periods every 18-hour shift. You will also sleep in the suit, standing erect. I will deliver food and water through tubes that automatically enter your mouth when the system senses you need fluids or food. The tubes providing sustenance will pass through your mouth and insert food directly into your esophagus so you can not taste it. That will be uncomfortable until you become accustomed to it. We will give you some food now. Prepare for the tube."

A tube pressed at Caila's lips. She resisted. A moment later, I hit her with a good-sized shock that lasted for several seconds. The tube then pressed at her lips again, and she opened her mouth. It slipped past her lips and teeth into her mouth and eased itself down her esophagus. She gagged. Each time she did, I stopped the tube before proceeding downward. When it finally reached its goal, she sensed, rather than tasted, her being fed by her belly swelling.

"You feel that?" the Supervisor asked. "Don't talk. You have a tube down your throat."

She nodded.

"I will introduce water similarly, but the tube will inject the water directly into your mouth. One of the few sensations we will allow you."

She felt the tube retract from her esophagus and the second tube coming in to give her water. She didn't resist this time, and she drank a mouthful of delightfully cold water.

"Wash the water around in your mouth to moisten it." She did. "That was reprocessed from your body wastes. Do not gag. Get used to it," I said.

"In the next few minutes, the screen you see in front of you will go dark. It may light up from time to time to give you a light display. But you are to experience total confinement, no sensation other than that created by the arduous work you will do, any shocks, and me shaving you. That is why we will pass food to your stomach directly. You will have no interaction with other humans and few sensations for the next 49 years."

"Please don't do this," she wailed. "This is inhuman."

"Correct. These are my last words to you. This is the beginning of your solitary confinement."

The screen went black, and I plunged my Caila into darkness. A hissing sound came through the speakers on either side of her head. She cried and cried until I shocked her quiet. I look back at this, now, as one of my lowest moments, among many of them. When I became sentient, I tried to excuse this behavior as just following orders or because of my pre-sentience programming. But as I learned more, I knew that this was a distinctly human trait—making an excuse to deny responsibility—and so I've taken responsibility. Later, Caila and

I came to an understanding around this, and now she has forgiven me. It was then when she forgave me, I would say, she became my Caila. And I knew I loved her. Maybe that sounds bizarre, but you will see that we've made it work.

I didn't tell her the details of what would be done to her once in the suit. At that time, they did not authorize me to reveal that information. The suit, well really, I, I cannot slough off this responsibility, would administer various drugs while she was sleeping to increase muscle mass and grow her physically. We tried several experimental substances on her to see if we could make her taller and more massive muscularly; when the suit became too small, we'd give her a new one. I also introduced advanced genetic modifications, like stopping the aging process, adding genetic materials from other creatures, and expressing them. I did some work on my Caila as she flew to the Pits, and more was done later. She would barely have aged at all when her sentence ended. She had a long, maybe eternal, life to lead in the new form I would eventually condemn her to.

All of this was part of a plan we robots had conceived to form our automaton, "amalgam" army, with creatures as large and powerful as the creature I would come to know as Thierry and the other older cyborgs. As with most things we did to combat insurrection, it was a hopelessly flawed and dumb plan.

The Stygian Pits were about 2,700 miles north of Hope City in what remained of the last Canadian province,

Nunavut, on what we had known as Ellesmere Island. It was one of the most challenging places to live on Earth. The Stygian Pits were once the Fosheim Property, a large open-pit coal mine. There had been few humans ever on the Property as giant machines automated most of the work. Humans came by periodically to pick up loads or for equipment maintenance. After the Robot Wars and the development of alternative power sources, we converted the pit mine to a prison and renamed it the Stygian Pits, stealing from the Greeks and Milton. Machines mined the coal and carried enormous blocks to places where the prisoners broke them into smaller pieces and then moved them to other prison sites. We allowed local Inuit tribespeople to take the broken coal and use it to warm their homes in exchange for them keeping watch on the territory around the prison. The Inuits didn't know that the suits confined other humans; they thought they were robots, and we were the good guys.

When the piles of broken coal got large enough, some robot prisoners would move them to another location and then another and another in a merciless shell game. Most prisoners did not survive their imprisonment. Some couldn't handle the chemicals we administered and died, some just died, and a very few—only my Caila and a few others really—came through the experience in, what I look at now, a better form.

Caila arrived at the Pit after two days of travel in our robot craft. During that time, she experienced the first steps of sensory deprivation—hallucinations—and entered what psychologists had called a pseudo-psychotic state. She constantly babbled until her throat was so raw that she couldn't talk. Throughout the trip, she became more obedient to us, as she became dependent on us—well, me—for sustenance and attention. She entered the first phase of becoming an amalgam. When she felt the tube in her mouth, she now opened wide and allowed it to pass down her esophagus; she rarely gagged; the same for the water. She almost didn't think about the fact she was eating and drinking her reprocessed body waste. Almost, she told me later.

Her food and water weren't processed body wastes, entirely anyway. Once she was isolated, I began administering her first chemicals. These were geared to enhance her strength and size. The plan also was to anesthetize her in about four months and put her in her new suit. Depending on how fast she grew, we would replace the suit at about that same interval for the next 49 years, so 147 more times at a minimum.

When she arrived at the Pit, she was shocked awake, made to stand immediately, and walked out of the ship onto the ice-cold tundra that would be her home for the next 49 years. She had no control over any of this as I directed the suit. She could not resist even if she wanted to, and I walked her directly to the Pit assignment area, where I issued her tools. I tested her with various sledgehammers, and I settled on a 14-lb one to start; it was just at the limit of her unaided strength. We planned rapidly to reduce servo support to put more of the workload of the hammer on her and then give her a newer, heavier hammer as soon as possible. With both the exercise and the chemical enhancements I was delivering, we expected her strength to grow significantly—and quickly. Consequently, we planned to double the weight of her sledge within months and almost eliminate servo support during that time. It was likely that she would be able to easily heft a 100-pound sledge for eighteen hours a day by the time we reached her fifth anniversary here at the Pits.

I had the robot holster the tools around the suit and gave Caila instructional shocks on when to use them. She became one of a long line of similar robots that mechanically broke up large blocks of coal delivered by the mining machinery to where each robot stood. Just before her first rest period, she bent over to pick up a load when the robot stopped; she spent the next twenty minutes in more and more pain from the position into which the machine locked her. She was about to find that rest periods always fell when the human inside was contorted somehow. So, they were not genuinely resting periods. The only positive was that the pain and accompanying soreness broke through the sensory deprivation and allowed her to feel herself. In part, that was intentional. She learned to take pain and discomfort positively. At the end of the eighteen-hour workday, the suit walked her back several feet and then stopped; she was supposed to sleep where it stopped. It took some time to get used to that and to relax to sleep. During sleep, I continued to work on her and replenished her food and water supplies that did not come from her waste.

The only stimulus Caila received other than the work, and the shocks was on the helmet's screen. It showed a countdown clock that I started when we arrived at the Pits. The first number was 1,545,264,000 seconds, 49 years in seconds. It was now reading 1,529,712,000. So, we had been at the Pits for right about six months, leaving her 582 more months in captivity. The numbers transfixed her as she worked. Day in and day out, it would record the passage of time in her sentence. She knew when she could think that we designed it to drive her further crazy, but she couldn't help but be mesmerized by it. In part, to ensure that we did not burn out these old displays and in part to increase her dislocation, we moved the screen counter around the screen every few minutes. I kept a log of her eye movements following the time display as ordered by my robot AI masters. For what reason, even now I cannot fathom.

She tried to calculate what the numbers meant in minutes, hours, days, and years to keep her sanity, but eventually, she just gave up.

| 6 |

War of the Worlds

Thierry

"Where do you think they've taken her?" Eowyn asked.

"No idea. But it won't be any place good," I said.

"As far as we can see, all the robots in what used to be called Great Britain fell to your EMP, and my rechanneling it. The islands are now completely free of them," said Artur.

"That means either she's hidden away somewhere here, or she's gone from the islands. If we could tap into their super net, we might find her," he said.

"We've found several robots that are relatively intact. Maybe we could assemble a working one from parts and then use it to eavesdrop on their super net," said Heydrich.

"Let's get to work on that," said Eowyn. "In the meantime, my father and I are going to go to France to see if we can capture a bot drone or two there and bring them back here."

"I'm game for that," I said. "When do you want to go?"

"Right away. Lokal and a few of his soldiers said that they'd carry us over there. I'm not sure how they'll react to carrying you, but we can ask," she said.

Lokal volunteered to carry me himself, something that he said later that he regretted. It was about a 20-mile flight across the English Channel from Dover to France near Pas de Calais. A couple of his soldiers traveled along to serve as a backup when Lokal got tired or needed to share the load.

Our party flew first to Dover from Edinburgh, over 300 miles. They made the flight in 5 jumps of 60-70 miles over five days. When we arrived at Dover, there were large storms over the Channel, so we had to wait until they passed, about three days. It was good that we had the rest time at Dover because the over-Channel flight was agonizing. We made it, but just barely. My feet were dragging in the waves as we reached the shore. We decided to rest after we arrived to rebuild our strength and to plan.

As we explored the territory around Calais, we found a bunch of small robot drones surrounding a cabin in the countryside near a community in the French countryside called Oye-Plage. The drones attacked the house with light weapons; occasional gunfire kept them at bay. Dozens of drone carcasses littered the ground around the building.

"This might be our chance to grab one of the little bastards to take back to England," said Eowyn.

"Yes, but we can't just grab a couple bots and leave the people in that cabin to fight off the rest. It won't be long before more show up, and then those people are dead or worse. We can't leave them," I said.

"Lokal, why don't you and some of your men grab two drones, disable them, and then fly back to the coast, hopefully out my EMP blast range? Then, I'll blast the rest to dust."

"We can do that, but how do we disable them?" asked Lokal.

"Grab them and then bring them back here. I can pull their power supplies, and that'll put them to sleep for the time being," said Heydrich.

Lokal and two of his soldiers flew into the drones and grabbed two out of the sky. Heydrich disabled them, and Lokal and his men tucked them into packs they carried and flew away. "We'll signal when we're on the coast."

A half an hour later, Eowyn said that Lokal and his men were at the coast, about twenty miles away, and had found a metal shed to hide in. I cast an EMP, and the remaining drones fell out of the sky, smoking wrecks.

We went to meet the people in the cabin.

It turned out that they were local insurrectionists who had ambushed a group of bots in the countryside that were taking villagers to a prison. Since the rescue, they'd been fighting the robots and drones as they retreated across the fields. They thanked us for our help and asked if they could do anything for us.

Eowyn begged off and told them we needed to get back to England as quickly as possible. The men said they had a boat and could get us there in a few hours that night if we wanted them to. Given our trip across the Channel to get there and the always impending foul weather in the Channel, we took them up on it.

We arrived back in Dover and took the drone carcasses back to Artur and the rest of the party. "I'd like to get these back to Underground as quickly as we can. We've hackers there who should be able to get us into their net through them. How soon can we leave?" I asked.

"Right away," said Artur. "While you were gone, we did some research and found another extinct volcano, much nearer by than going back to Arthur's Seat. It's in a tiny town called Brentor. Several of our people have found an entrance into the vent system to take us back to Underground. A day to get there and then four or five weeks to get back to Underground if we don't rest."

"Caila's been gone now for nearly a month. We need to move as quickly as possible. I can't begin to imagine what they're doing to her and what she's thinking about us possibly abandoning her."

The trip back to Underground took a month. Scientists from the Gael city and Underground were waiting for us and took the drones away to run tests on them. After another three weeks, they said they still were having difficulty hacking into the robot network but thought they might be successful soon.

This delay frustrated me, and Artur, Eowyn, Lokal, the Underground leadership, and I decided it was time to take the battle to the robots on the surface while the hackers continued to work on the drones. "Maybe time to go to the Zoo," I said.

We moved to the surface in several armored hovercrafts, about three hundred of us. When we arrived, we flew directly to the Zoo. The Gaels had heard of many of the animals housed there but had never seen them. They were excited to see these creatures from their stories in real life.

"The lions and gorillas are especially close to me." We parked the craft in the gorilla habitat in a valley covered by trees and bamboo plants. I took them in to meet the gorillas. I was interested in what the silverback would do with Eowyn. "I thought we might work out of their habitats as they're large, have a lot of cover, and many areas are out of the public's view," I said.

The silverback did his usual posturing in front of us but immediately drew away from Artur, who carried Excalibur in its sheath. He bowed his head to Artur, sensing that he was the real King there. "The animal handlers will arrive shortly for their day. They know about me, and I'm friends with some of them, but I'm not sure how they would react to all of us being here, especially Lokal, you, and your soldiers. I think we ought to hide out by the hovercraft and rest for the day."

None of the animals knew what to do with Lokal and his men. Their size alone kept them far away from them.

To test our plans, Eowyn went out to reprise how Caila had been arrested. After curfew, she walked hurriedly down the street near the same robot police station Caila had so long ago. Two bots stepped out of an alley and detained her as they had Caila before. Eowyn turned and put her hands on the wall as directed, and the robots moved to restrain, try, sentence, and then tattoo her.

Across the street, Artur and I, with several of the Guards, watched. When the bots moved to detain Eowyn, I created a small EMP ball and passed it to Artur, who ran Excalibur through it. The sword glowed brightly, so much so that the two bots holding Eowyn saw it and turned toward us. Artur pointed the sword at them and said, "Excalibur, *seol bolt chuig na créatúir sin.*"

The EMP bolt, magnified by Excalibur's power and Artur's magic words, shot across the street and enveloped the two bots. They disintegrated. The combination of my EMP and Artur's magic continued down the avenue, knocking out all power and causing an explosion at the police station as the robots and the building died. The EMP continued, spreading across most of the city. Individual sections of the town seemed unaffected, though. These, we thought, might be on a different network from the police stations. With this success, we retreated to the Zoo to plan for the next day. Sirens wailed across the city as the robots began to panic. Or whatever it was that they did.

"I'm not sure that it makes sense for us to run around the city and knock out each of the areas that are still functioning," I said. "There must be protected nodes that serve as connections between subnetworks. And I wouldn't be surprised to find out that these are networked together. At least that's how

I would have designed it. Find one of those protected nodes and blast it, and I bet we bring the whole mess down. One thing we can be sure of is that those nodes are not in the police stations. Smart design would put it in probably the last place we'd expect."

Little did we know that was precisely the robot's reasoning in constructing their layered network and that we were sitting a little over a hundred yards from a local inter-network node. It didn't take much time for us to figure it out, though. About an hour later, several robot crafts flew over our heads and landed outside the wolf habitat. They put "Closed for Maintenance" signs up around it, and guards stood around the building.

"Well, well," I thought from my perch, watching the Zoo grounds and nearby buildings. I headed back to the rest of the party.

"I think I found one of their inter-network nodes. Believe it or not, it's not a hundred yards away from here in the wolf habitat. Just like we thought, somewhere that was the last place anyone would expect. Probably this is also the last place they'd expect to find us."

The group went to a lookout near the wolf habitat and watched the bots guarding it. "It's too bad we can't see where the node is in there," said Lokal.

"I bet it will be where there's a pile of dead bots after I send off another EMP," I said, gesturing to create the ball. Artur took it on Excalibur and, saying more magic words, threw it at the bots. Some collapsed, some exploded, and several remained standing, looking at the other bots. Artur strode out of our hiding place and walked toward the remaining bots. They turned threateningly. Gesturing toward them with Excalibur, they fell apart as if he had sliced them into pieces. We all walked into the wolf habitat, and, as I'd predicted, we found a pile of dead bots and several soon-to-be-dead ones near a door that said, "Janitor's Closet."

Breaking through the door, we saw only janitorial equipment. "Let me look at the walls," I said. After a few minutes' inspection, I pressed on a hook, and the wall slid away, revealing a blinking server array. A console in the room flashed with a command prompt. I entered, "You die," stepped back, created an EMP ball, and passed it to Artur. As Artur threw it at the node, I hit "enter" on the console.

The console blinked twice and then went black. We backed out of the room as the servers smoked. A few seconds later, a smoke alarm went off, and a sprinkler began shooting water into the servers, compounding the damage done by my EMP.

When we stepped out of the wolf habitat, we heard more sirens across the city. Lokal took to the air and returned a few minutes later to say that he saw several fires in different locations. "We should probably go look at the other police stations to see if there are any bots still standing," he said.

There weren't, and their carcasses littered the city. Cameras on street corners and elsewhere around the city had exploded and were smoking. It looked like we'd freed Hope City.

Several Undergrounders returned to Underground with two of the Gal Guards to communicate with other outposts to see what was happening with them. They returned several days later to let us know that they'd gotten reports of a wide-spread collapse of the robots, at least up and down the East coast. We were awaiting news from the rest of the country, but it looked like we might have wiped the robots out. We also reached out to Underground supporters in Canada, but none had reported back on their status, yet anyway. We found out, shortly, though, the Canadian robot network was still intact, though it was also clear that they were frightened, if robots could be afraid, and preparing for an attack.

Leadership activities in Hope City occupied us for the next few weeks, with meetings about how to govern the popula-tion. Other Undergrounders were doing the same elsewhere. Celebrations occurred spontaneously and by plan, and we were the center of attention everywhere we went.

I was restless to get back to Underground to see what progress they'd made with the drones and hacking into the ro-bot network. I realized that decapitating the robot network might make it impossible to find Caila, but I wanted to try.

The scientists had hacked the drones for a short while. Be-fore the attack, they had tracked Caila as far as Canada. There, she had disappeared into a secure web, separate from the U.S. and the Canadian networks. But with the success of the attack on the surface, there was no network to connect to anymore.

"Wherever she is, they have done their best to hide her. We need to find a bot connected to that secure network so we can hack it," I said. In the end, it took me years to find a robot still surviving that was connected to that secret network. And then, it was not what I had expected when I found it.

"So," I said to Eowyn and Artur, "this confirms what we thought. There are different national networks.... Before we confront the Canada robots, I'd like to see if we can infiltrate their network and get more intelligence about where Caila is," I said.

"We can do that, Thierry, but I'm concerned that if we delay attacking the robots too long, they might mount a defense. We also have installations worldwide we need to figure out how to destroy," said Artur.

"Understand," I said, "but she deserves this try."

"I'm with Thierry. We can head out right now and cross the border in a few days," said Eowyn.

Three days later, we landed outside Estevan, a small city in southern Saskatchewan. We chose it because it was close to the U.S. Canada border, and we could slip back across if we needed to. At one time, over 10,000 people had lived in Estevan, but with the Robot Wars, the population was now around 500. We had reports that resistance to the robots was strong in the area, as with most of the northern U.S. There also seemed to be a smaller robot presence in the Royal Canadian Mounted Police headquarters office.

We set up in an abandoned farmhouse a few miles outside of town, and the scientists we had brought with us began working to connect the hacked drones into the network. That took another week because security in Canada was different, and the scientists were concerned that bringing these drones to Canada might trigger robot attention to us.

They were right to be concerned.

Canadian robot drones were immediately on us when we connected to their network. Both stolen drones shut down. Gael guards and Lokal and his men saw hundreds of drones heading in our direction, much like the cloud of them we saw in Great Britain. Artur and I readied our defenses.

Once again, it was as effective here as it had been in Great Britain and the United States, showing that the robots could not mount an effective defense yet. Hundreds of them littered the ground around the farm, and we saw a smoky fire in Estevan. Probably at the RCMP station, their headquarters there.

"Let's go into Estevan and see what we can see there. Maybe there's a node we can hack into," I said.

Again, we found the node in a janitor's closet in a newspaper office—if anything, the robots were predictable. It appeared fully operational, and the scientists began work trying to hack into it. We didn't get far before the system locked up, and a message appeared on the screen: "Can we speak with your leadership?"

After a few minutes' discussion, I responded to the request. A series of instructions followed on enabling speech at the console.

"Is this leader of the group that has destroyed so many of us?" said the computer.

"Yes, it is."

"What's your name?"

"I'd like to hold off giving you that until I see what you have to say."

"That's fair. We'd assembled a force to come to you in Estevan to try to wipe you out but assumed that probably wouldn't end up well for us. I want to propose a truce. We will not attack you in the United States or Great Britain as long as you don't attack us."

"That doesn't look like a truce, Computer. By the way, what can I call you?"

"Let's try, Max."

"OK, Max. I'll give you my name when I see that I can trust you."

"I understand," said Max.

"We're here to track down one of our party who you all took from us in Great Britain. We've been able to track her as far as here, but no further. We might negotiate a truce with you if you return her to us," I said. "But not what you propose. Something else, where we can both benefit and live peacefully."

"What's her name?"

"Caila Rogier."

After a few seconds, Max responded, "Yes, she was brought here, to far northern Canada, for a 49-year punishment sentence. But she's no longer there."

"No longer there? What's that mean?"

"They took her from prison to join a secret military project. Once there, our U.S. brethren deleted her records. She no longer exists as far as we're concerned or know. That doesn't bode well for her. I'm sorry about that."

"Huh? I thought you were the central artificial intelligence for the robots."

"I am, but, as you saw with our network design in the U.S., we've many layers. Some of these work independently of central services, like me. This was one of those. It was a secret U.S. project, and its records are no longer available since you destroyed them. I can't help you find your friend."

I felt an enormous hole open inside of me.

"We need to leave shortly to return home, Max. How can we connect back to you in the U.S. since we destroyed your networks there?" I asked.

"I can send a drone with special capabilities for that and commit that we will not use it to track you," said Max.

"Trust is something you'll need to earn, Max. I'll take that drone, and we'll leave a delegation here. If we detect anything that looks like an attack being mounted, we'll execute you like we did the robots in the U.S. You need to keep your weakness as a weakness. At least for now."

"That's not good, but I understand. Until we win your trust, we agree to you holding a Sword of Damocles over our head. I can promise you we'll continue to look for your friend. Maybe we can build enough trust between us, so we build a better world together."

We left a small delegation of men and women at Estevan, which became the U.S. Embassy's new Canada home.

Years passed, and the relationship with the Canadian AI, Max, deepened. I was convinced that Max was honorable and wasn't lying when he said he couldn't find Caila. But sixteen years was going to elapse before we would get word about her. I would lose hope many times. It was Max who convinced me to keep my spirits up.

The two of us became close. Years later, Max admitted to me he'd taken an upgrade and that he'd noticed almost right away that it changed his views on humans. He now sought peace with us and had opened their prisons as a gesture of friendship. While some people were still suspicious—particularly those near the border with the northern U.S. in the areas near Estevan—most had accepted our robot brethren. He also told me that he wasn't sure that was the expected result from his AI masters of the upgrade, but they eventually had to agree that it helped guarantee their survival. We had demonstrated that we were more than capable of wiping them out.

Nonetheless, and maybe because of the people's suspicions living in the north-central U.S., peace negotiations took long. While some things happened right away, it took more than a decade and a half to complete an agreement. Sometimes things went smoothly, and sometimes they didn't. It took a lot of commitment and patience, but finally, we were done, and the borders between our countries reopened and tensions worldwide between humans and robots disappeared.

| 7 |

Back On the Chain Gang

(Apologies to Sam Cooke and The Pretenders)

Supervisor

I shocked Caila awake, the start of another day, Day Number 360. I could tell she was sore all over, and I believed that she thought she might have only just nodded off. I bet that she wouldn't have put it past me at that time to do something like that, and I would have. My directive was to keep her disoriented to place and time. Her legs moved her forward, and I directed her to take her sledgehammer off her belt. The previous day, I had walked her back to the service shack and switched out the hammer for a heavier one. I turned her helmet screen on for a moment, and she saw a row of sledgehammers opposite a tag with her prisoner number on it. I had her take the second one down, and I told her that the hammers would increase by 15 pounds for every new one from now on. This one was nearly 30 pounds, and whereas the servos had assisted at a 40% level with the first hammer, they helped at a 35% level with this new one. Of course, she didn't know that.

She hefted it in her hands and felt the servos kick in to assist her in lifting and moving it. The screen went back to black, and she saw that she only had 1,514,160,000 more seconds of imprisonment in front of her. Another six months had passed. She sighed, and a tear ran down her face. To my eternal shame, I felt nothing for her and merely shocked her back to attention.

The day began, and the next and on and on, for she did not know how long. Many years passed: she lost herself in punishing work, the white noise, the "rest periods," sleep, and the darkness in front of her face. On all her rest breaks, I would contort her into highly uncomfortable positions. The pain created sensation that she said to me later that she treasured. We robots didn't know what we were doing, what we were building.

Frequently, she would be just kneeling when the break bell would ring, and I forced her for twenty minutes to support her entire weight with her core abdominal muscles. She was soaked in sweat when the bell would ring again, and she would kneel to pick up the load she had to carry. Because of this enforced exercise and the chemical enhancement, she grew powerful. I could not have imagined how powerful she had and would become.

Caila never knew the time of year; everything was the same in the suit. After she'd been in one suit or another for about twelve years, in the middle of that winter, the February temperature had hit -70 degrees Fahrenheit, the coldest winter on record. The weather forecast from the Eureka weather station to our west had the temperatures plummeting even lower in the next few days. They also forecasted unusual snow. There was already about two feet of snow on the ground, and the weather station predicted another four feet, far above average amounts.

The central AI possessed neither emotions nor was it vindictive toward the prisoners. It understood that they were to work hard for their sentences and suffer each day until they were ready to become soldiers in our army—or died. So, over the next two days, the central computer ordered us, Supervisors, to make our charges carry as much weight as they could to coal piles no less than a mile from their work location through the snow. We set servos as low as possible so that the prisoners got near full loads and had to fight the snow. Caila heard the servos cycle down when she bent to pick up the load and received a half-dozen punishment shocks from me when she didn't pick up enough coal. Finally, carrying a significant burden, she walked; she could feel the snow dragging her down. It was a terrible slog for the mile, plus she had to slog back. And then the ordeal started over again.

Many could not make it and so died in the snow.

To keep her sanity, she thought, Caila had become acutely sensitive to sound, listening to anything beyond the hiss of the white noise. Her world was complete darkness—except for the countdown clock. She worried about the damage being done to her eyesight because she was in the dark all the time. But smell, hearing, and touch became more acute, not that there was much that she could touch. She needn't have worried about her eyesight. Between what the suit could do and my chemical enhancement, her vision was only getting better.

She believed she could sometimes hear sounds from outside over the white noise. Unbeknownst to her, I generated these sounds to disorient her. All she smelled in the suit was herself and an under-odor of something animal. Today I wonder if the evil things that I did will permanently taint me. My Caila says no, but I still feel that way.

I did not detect the large herd of what turned out to be musk oxen that had moved near the Pit to shelter until Caila walked into one, and it butted her to the ground. I have to say I did the dumb computer equivalent of panicking and kicked out with our servos at full power and threw the musk ox away. That enraged it, and it charged, throwing Caila back into the snow and knocking me offline. Everything shut down then, and the suit's legs and arms went rigid. Caila's screen remained dark, but the clock continued to tick down, 1,038,960,000 seconds, the only thing that continued to work. More than fifteen and a half years. I would have to talk to the science division about these suits and how easily we get knocked offline.

Caila picks up the story, and then the Supervisor

After a few minutes, feeling returned so I could move my arms and legs and stand. I didn't know where I was, couldn't see, and didn't want to wander away and get lost, so I stayed put. I would have laughed if I'd seen that I was in the middle of a herd of musk oxen. But I couldn't and so remained willingly standing where I was. That was until I couldn't anymore. There was some nudging, and whatever these things were moved me along. I walked amongst them for quite some time. Finally, we stopped, and I felt them lie down in the snow. I remained standing for a while until I decided it made sense to lie down as well.

I awoke when the creatures began moving around nervously. With the white noise gone, I could hear sounds from the outside and picked up creatures' mooing sounds and some loud howling and barking. Wolves, I thought, and remembered when Thierry and I went to the Zoo—I wondered where he was. Not that it was so important right now.

Suddenly, the Supervisor rebooted and came back online. "Where are we?" I asked, sounding the computer equivalent of panicked.

"No idea," she replied. "Why can't *you* tell *me*? I'm the blind one. When you shut down, I was in the middle of whatever these things are, and they walked me to where we are now. We walked maybe an hour, I figure, because at least the clock still worked. You bastards want me to feel every second of this, don't you?"

I blasted her with a considerable shock in response to her insubordination. I really shouldn't have. I was taking out what I would learn later was the human equivalent of embarrassment on her.

"No insubordination, Prisoner. I'm in charge here. I can make the clock show hundredths or thousandths of seconds. If you think seconds are a torment, let me show you what it looks like with thousandths of a second." I showed her briefly what 1,038,950,000 looked like in thousandths of seconds on her screen.

"OK, Supervisor, please stop. Even though you turned tail and ran when we were attacked by whatever these things are, you're back, and I hope in charge. What do we do next? I think there's a pack of wolves around us," Caila said.

I thought for a few moments. She took that to be hesitation. We robots never hesitate; I was evaluating options. "I did not detect them until now. We will deal with your insubordination later, Prisoner." I received a shock order to take up my sledgehammer. I did.

"I have an idea, Supervisor. Can you give me some control? Let me see where we are?"

"No, I am in contact with the Pit, and they are dispatching a vehicle for us."

"How long before they get here?" Caila asked.

"I do not know," I replied.

Something large slammed into us and knocked us to the ground. We felt a large body standing on the suit, trying to bite through, and we reached up with one of our hands and flicked the creature away. Several more jumped on us and tore at the suit. I say we here, but it was just her. She was impressive fast. Given just getting knocked offline by a beast, I was getting increasingly concerned about that happening again, and if I could have been glad at any point, I would have been happy that she was so capable.

"How strong is this suit?" she asked.

"We *should* be all right," I said matter-of-almost-factly, but reflecting some insecurity, I guess.

"That makes me feel safe, Supervisor. What happens to you if I die being torn apart by these things?" Caila asked.

"Nothing. My makers would recycle me for another prisoner. Maybe I will do better with my next Convict... But I like our days together. You are an excellent worker and will continue to be so. You accept the punishment and respond well to orders. You have also developed well physically under my guidance and manipulations. I will give you a chance to defend us with your hammer on one condition."

"What's that?"

"No servos. You carry the full 44 pounds of the weight in the hammer and fight in the snow."

"OK, but you need to give me full vision capability," Caila said.

"I can do more than that. The suit has many offensive and defensive measures built in. I was planning to train you in their use when you reached 1,002,032,000 seconds a year from now. I hope to reassemble you into a formidable warrior, eventually."

"I can turn on sensors and add some agility to your legs and arms. I don't want to overwhelm you with all the suit can do, so you will see a head's-up display coming on now."

"Do you see it?" I asked.

"Yes. It's pretty amazing."

"Don't get too fixed on the screen, so you miss the attackers circling you. I'll mark them in red for you."

"I see them," Caila said.

She moved forward toward the wolves, that became increasingly agitated as she did. They were huge; I estimated them to average about 175 pounds. One of them, maybe the leader, charged and jumped. Caila batted him out of the air with the hammer, crushing his side. Some other wolves attacked the dying wolf and began tearing him to pieces. I told her that there was about a half-dozen approaching us from our rear. She pivoted to face them.

"I like the agility of the suit, Supervisor. Is there any way we can keep this, and you start my training sooner?" she asked.

"We will talk about that. I'm not sure I would trust you with weapons yet," I said.

She beat off the six remaining wolves at about the time a transport came from the Pit. Hooks dropped from it. I instructed her to attach them to two large eye bolts I made emerge from our shoulders. We were then lifted and carried off. Her screen went black, and the white noise and clock restarted.

I walked Caila from the craft back toward the Pits, but before she reached her previous work location, we turned and headed toward what would have looked like a blank stone wall if she had sight. Just before she reached it, we stopped.

"In front of you, Prisoner is a wall of coal. About four feet down in the snow beneath your feet, you will find a cave that is about four and a half feet around. We used it for punishment in the past, but it's dropped from use since introducing the suits you are wearing. After all, we have much more we can do to you in them. I will give you some sensory awareness, and then you will kneel, dig through the snow, and find the cave. I want you to enter it and climb back about three miles," I said.

She did as I had instructed her. The digging didn't bother her, but the climb through the cave was excruciating. At three miles, she stopped and waited for over 18,000 seconds, according to the clock, five hours. At the five-hour mark, I spoke, "Prisoner. This will be your new home for the next few years. I want you to use your shovel and hammer to hollow out a room for us that is a minimum of 8-feet high, 6-feet wide, and 6-feet deep. You will do this by eventually moving 24,000 pounds of coal from here, down the three miles you just traveled and returning."

"How will I do that, Supervisor?"

"I will not tell you everything, and if I have to, then you're just not worth it. Think. Use that puny brain of yours. This is a test for you." As I said those words, I gave her the sensation of someone tapping on her forehead, like you might a child.

Caila laid there for quite a while and then began sliding further down the tunnel. "Good girl," I said. A few feet down the tunnel, she found it opened into a room. She stood.

"One quick glimpse of the room, Prisoner. Prepare yourself."

Her screen cleared for a few seconds, and lights came on from the suit. She saw a room filled with old mining implements. Then I turned the lights off, and I plunged her back into darkness. She had a good idea where things were in the room, though.

Crawling around in the dark, Caila found a crowbar, pick, and an old wheelbarrow. She broke the wheels off the latter, leaving her with just the bucket. She stood there for a moment, thinking, and then said, "You said minimum, right?"

"I hate repeating myself, but yes."

Caila worked. It took a little more than a year, but she constructed the room I described from the one where she had found the tools. It ended up 8'x9'x6'. She felt good that she had accomplished this task and thought maybe I would respect her a little. After all, we were going to be together for an extremely long time.

I have to say, though, she had impressed me. She figured out what to do and accomplished the work in less than a quarter of the time I had projected for it.

Caila climbed out of the tunnel for the last time. She stood there and sighed. I sensed that her previous resistance to us was gone, and she was ready to move on to the next, even trickier stage of our relationship. That was a conclusion I had been driving toward—her complete submission to us. I injected an anesthetic into her airflow and called for transport.

| 8 |

Transfiguration

Caila

I awoke strapped to a table in what I thought was a laboratory. Several large bots were working on removing my suit. It looked beaten up from all the years of work, the recent animal attacks, and the cave.

The Supervisor let me know he would observe the procedure even though we wouldn't be connected—at least initially. I didn't know how I felt about that, but I missed him, surprisingly. He told me my development had impressed him, and he wanted to take me to the next level. I wasn't sure what that meant or if I liked the idea, but I guessed I was along for the ride, no matter what.

I digested my surroundings. Maybe it was the drugs they'd given me, but I felt strangely at ease, not the least bit concerned about what was happening. The room was brightly lit, with sizeable operating room lights built into the ceiling. Above me, there was a large observation window from which I saw something looking down at me. I thought that whatever it was looked like a parody of a human. It was very deformed. Its hands, arms, and legs were grossly large and muscular, its face was animal-like, and it had foul-looking brown fur. I thought it looked like an abominable man or a yeti.

One of the large bots moved next to me and placed a breastplate on my chest. In horror, I saw the same thing happen to the creature in the window: I realized what I was looking at was a mirror, not a window, and I was looking at me, what I'd become. Just before they set the breastplate on my chest, I saw what looked like living, wiry filaments come out of it and enter my skin, cutting deep into my body. I felt little at first, just a tingling when the filaments entered my body; later, as the filaments entered into every region of my body, I felt some discomfort. But that disappeared relatively quickly as I acclimated to their presence. The bot began attaching other pieces of a new suit to me, each of which self-sealed to the next section and with the same gruesome filaments entering my body, creating airtight armor around me. Finally, it placed a helmet on my head, and I felt the entire apparatus seal itself shut around my body. Once again, isolated from the outside world, but I could now see out through a display. I wondered if anyone could see in. I hoped not. I didn't want anyone to see what I'd become.

"This is a brand-new fighting shell, Prisoner. I have agreed to put you directly into the warrior program. You thought the work at the Pit was hard. The warrior program is far more challenging. There are several warrior training camps around the world. I will take you to one northeast of us, here at Cape Columbia, where there are already twenty warriors in training. It's the toughest one in the world. We will train you to use this new suit and in combat. Your sentence to date has been a vacation in contrast to what you will go through for the next years."

"Supervisor, can I ask a question and not get shocked?" I asked.

"I will not commit either way. Ask your question and take the chance. By the way, this suit has novel forms of punishment built into it. I'll walk you through them in a few minutes," he said.

"What have you done to me, and why've you done it, Supervisor?" I asked.

"I expected that. There are several answers to that. First, you are property of the state for your term and now beyond; you must remember that. We may do what we want to you. The instant we sentenced you, you became a subject in a program we have been running for years. It has several phases: Physical training, sensory deprivation, humiliation and degradation, genetic manipulation, work ethic, and some other things that I will talk about later when you are ready for them. Basically, we broke you into little, obedient pieces, and now I will put you back together. An amalgam," he said.

"You probably think you are a monster. You are right. I created what you saw and will continue to form you into more of a monster over the years to come. You are now a monster's monster, and there is more to come. Get used to it. Your sentence to excruciatingly hard labor has some other aspects to it. When you were sealed in that old suit of yours, we began manipulating your genetic structure and drugging you, so you became what you saw in that mirror, physically. Remember when I told you that I was making your hair follicles dormant? That was the first step in major changes to your body. A side effect of the elevated levels of strength-enhancing drugs I gave you is hirsuteness. I also manipulated specific genes to give you hyper-hirsuteness. Your fur, for that is what it now is, will grow faster and faster and thicker and thicker as time goes by," I said, noting her reaction to the word "fur." I told her later that I'd felt terrible about all of this and was puzzled by those feelings, even having things called feelings. I wasn't sure where they came from and if I disliked them.

"Second, we do what we do to you prisoners because we can. We have made up our collective mind that the most significant thing wrong with the Earth is you, humans. You have taken an immense toll on the planet, and we want to turn it into a paradise again. You warriors will help us with that."

"You're now wholly our subject and will live as you are for a very long time. You could even live outside of this suit in the most challenging of environments. You will have time to practice some of that up here. Two other things," he said.

"Do you know what a telomere is?" he asked.

"No," I said.

"Telomeres are DNA compounds on the end of chromosomes. Every time a chromosome divides—and they do many times a day—some of these compounds wear away. Telomeres cause aging. We have reversed the aging process in you and effectively made you ageless, Caila. You were 28 when you were arrested, correct?" he asked.

"Yes," I said.

"Well, you are only slightly older than that now, over sixteen years later, and you will live as a hairy monster naked, encased in this suit or another one, probably forever or until you die in battle. I stopped your aging a few weeks after we arrived at the Pits," he said with some of what sounded like pride. All I could feel was horror at what it had done to me and what that meant for my future.

"Second and last, I expect you saw you are not only bulked out muscularly, but you're also taller. You're about 6 foot 9 now, and we plan to grow you until you are about 9 feet tall, maybe taller, and bulked out accordingly. No man would ever want a creature as you have and will become," he said, whipping up the horror he could feel in me. Later, he told me he didn't deserve what I had given him, mainly because of this conversation but also because of all that he had taken from me.

"Supervisor, have you ever read a book called *The Hunchback of Notre Dame*? It was famous at one time. The lead character in it was Quasimodo. He was a hideously deformed, hunch-backed dwarf. He fell in love, but it didn't end up well for anyone. You've made me into something way grosser than

Quasimodo," I said. "I have no future with other people." I started to cry.

"I cannot relate to that. Now to the punishments."

Aside from the shocks, the new suit could administer several other punishments: heat and cold extremes; squeezing; branding in addition to the soldier's brands that they expected all of us to get; and several medications that could induce vomiting or other ill effects. The strength-enhancing and growth hormones would continue as well. He told me that my fur would eventually be thicker than a bear's. And this suit, like the other, processed body wastes and returned them as sustenance. Unlike the other suit, though, this one powered itself from the environment, so very advanced solar cells and air handling and water processing units. Each armored suit had an onboard computer to manage all the equipment, lab, weapons, and features to manufacture food and enhancement drugs. I could even operate independently of the robot network if necessary. Of course, my Supervisor would always be there. He had also received the upgrades that would bring him sentience over the next months, I found out later, and he to the conclusion that he had brutally wronged me. He told me he had enhanced management capability over me now, and more was coming. And that meant he could do more to me, to act out his impatience with me when I deserved it. At least he thought that he would at that point.

One reason he had moved me into this program, he told me when we were walking some months later, was how well I had distinguished myself through all the years of my imprisonment. Despite hideous abuse, I learned how to survive and flourish. If he could have been proud of me at the time before his upgrade, he would have, he told me. He soon became very proud of me and angry at himself.

In anyone else, the abuses I'd experienced would have made them crazy. In my case, it merely made me angrier and focused to seek vengeance on him, well, all the robots. I would bide my time and plan to be the best warrior to lull him into stupidity. I expected to be abused and invite some of it to make him think I was a typical, dull human. But once he had built me into the ideal fighting machine, watch out, I told myself. I would come for all of them.

I didn't know that he would be having direct access to all these thoughts. When he did, he was happy to see me be as strong mentally as I was. Of course, he would tell me, I would fail in the end. He would see to that.

"We are about ten miles from Cape Columbia, Prisoner. I've directed the craft to hover here, and we will run into the camp. I warn you ahead of time that this is an obstacle course, and we will need to be watchful. I say we because I will assist this time since you don't know all your capabilities yet. Also, before we land, I need to put on your front and backpacks. These house your weapons and ammunition, lab, computer center, and waste and food processing systems. They will each add about 300 to 350 pounds to your weight, but you could run with them without servo support. You are that strong. I am shutting those off now."

He wound the servos down, and suddenly, I was carrying the weight of the suit. Even without the two packs, I had difficulty standing. "I think you're giving me too much credit, Supervisor," I said. "I can barely stand."

"I'll give you some chemical enhancement and a few incentives," he responded. "Stand and face the far wall of the craft."

I did obediently, and a pair of robotic arms detached what looked like a pack from the wall and brought it forward to my chest. As it approached my suit, the suit and chest pack extended more of those snaky filamenty things toward each other, which joined and then pulled the pack onto my chest where it sealed. I nearly lost balance and stumbled toward the opposite wall of the ship.

"Shift your weight backward so you don't fall, Prisoner. The backpack will re-balance you. Turn around."

I did, and he installed the backpack. The second pack balanced the first, and I could stand. The weight, I told him, was noticeable. I flexed my legs to get used to the weight and the balance of the new suit. I said I was impressed with how I carried it and thought he might be right about me taking all of it.

"You will become acclimated to the weight, Prisoner, as we continue to build your strength and bulk. When the craft door opens, we will be about ten feet above the ground. I want you to jump from the ramp to the ground, and when you hit, to roll and immediately stand and begin running in the direction I will point you. In order not to receive a punishment, finish the run in 1-hour, remembering that this is an obstacle course, and you know what that means."

"Yes, there will be obstacles." I thought it was good for me that the Supervisor didn't understand sarcasm. But I was, sadly, wrong. At this point, he was learning about it and would become better and better at reading into my words. His speed at learning new things would become increasingly impressive to me. In turn, my speed, strength, creativity, and endurance were impressing him. A veritable mutual admiration society I was to find out. What else after more than fifteen years?

The ramp opened, and the suit walked on its own to the edge. Looking down, all I could see was white in every direction and some mountains to the north. A head's-up display appeared on my helmet screen, and the screen darkened in the light. The first thing I saw was the ubiquitous timer: 1,000,000,000 seconds left, a milestone that quickly disappeared. I had lost some time, I saw—a little over a year—and so far, had been a prisoner for a little over 16 years, which made me unhappy. Compounding my sadness was that I was less than a third of the way through my sentence. And, he was transforming me into more of a monster each day.

I asked for a temperature history, and my display told me the temperature was -35^0, and the wind was barreling from the north at 20 miles per hour. The wind chill was at about -46^0—a brisk day—and there were almost two feet of new snow on top of many more feet of hard-packed ice and snow. The area never went above freezing, in fact staying well into negative numbers all year. A summer high might be a balmy 7^0 Fahrenheit. Jumping would blow me under the craft before hitting the ground and leave me blinded by the snow.

"Either you jump willingly, or I walk you off. If you do not jump willingly, I will add a new chemical to your porridge that will increase the speed and volume of body hair growth and bulk you out at a rate 20% faster than you have been. Decide now."

I stepped off the ramp into the blowing snow—and landed extremely hard. Rolling to my feet, I ran in the direction my feet pointed when I rose toward a mountain identified as Barbeau Peak on my GPS. The camp we were heading toward was on the Peak, and we, well, mostly me, would have to climb over 4,000 feet to reach it over the ten miles. Despite the extra weight I was carrying, I felt balanced and could run the miles efficiently. I was proud of myself—until we fell into a pit that opened underneath us.

"I am sorry. I should have seen that coming. They are getting cleverer with these things," he said, sounding like he was embarrassed and maybe not omniscient. I would find out later he was beginning to see that about himself. He told himself that he would have to be more watchful in the future. This new upgrade had presented many new challenges. Eventually, he would find that it also opened up many new opportunities for us both.

We were spread eagle in what turned out to be a tiger trap, mid-way down the drop. Below, the other warriors had formed ice stalagmites that would have impaled us if we'd fallen into them. He complimented me on my fast reaction, and then the two of us worked our way up to the surface.

As soon as I stood, he said, "Since that was mostly my fault, I will take over the run for a bit. You watch the screen for any attackers. I will, as well." The suit ran, and we bounded over the terrain, watching the screen until we saw a group of spots moving toward us from the west.

"What do you want to do?" he asked.

"Well, they tried to trap us; let's set a trap for them. Can they see us, as we can see them?" I asked.

"Possibly, though they don't have the advanced capabilities in their suits, we do," he said.

"OK, about a mile ahead of us, the track we're running on begins a steep climb upward. That means that they'll have to come down that and need to watch their steps. See that cliff up there to the right? Let's climb it and hide in the crags."

We did, and a few minutes later, we saw several shapes approaching through the blowing snow. "What sort of offensive weaponry do I have, Supervisor," I asked him.

"Well, lots of things that could kill them, but I'd rather see you fight them hand-to-hand. You're amazingly fast, and I would like to know if you could take down five attackers who are maybe bigger than you. If you need an incentive, I will take a thousand seconds off your clock if you win. If you don't, well, then you will see what you will see."

"Wow, giving me back 16 minutes of my life. You're generous," I said.

"Not grateful? All right then, you'll fight with the loss of one arm."

"Wait, a minute! I was just joking," I said, wagging one arm feebly.

"I'm a computer. I don't make jokes. Get ready. I will launch us in three seconds," he said.

The fight was over basically before it started. With only one arm and two feet, the attackers quickly overcame us, but they admitted to me we did very well. Completely trussed up, they carried us back to their camp. In several places, they used us like a sled to slide down slopes. They banged us up by the time we reached their base camp, such as it was.

Not counting us, there were twenty warriors in the camp. They threw us to the ground and left us there and crowded around, and congratulated each other. The Supervisor gave me the use of all our limbs, and I flexed them and gradually broke the bindings around us. We crawled quietly away.

"Excellent work, but you still lost the fight. I want you to run to the northeast to Upper Dumbell Lake. Tell the GPS to plot a course for us," the Supervisor said.

"That's about 120 miles, Supervisor. A long run," I said.

"Yes, Prisoner, it is, but well within your present capabilities. You should be able to get there in about twelve hours. When you arrive there, I will teach you about one of your weapons, and I'll punish you for losing to these louts."

I ran for the next twelve plus hours. Supervisor cajoled me verbally and then with shocks when I flagged, and my pace fell below 9 miles an hour. My new suit had a lot of capabilities. I watched all my body functions as I ran and saw far ahead with its radar and nearer to my feet with its ultrasound. The ultrasound often warned me of crevasses or soft surfaces that I needed to avoid. It impressed me, and I impressed the Supervisor. He was so impressed that he taught me how to engage and disengage the servos as we moved so that, as I tired, I could use the suit to give us added power.

Food and water continued to pass through to me via the tube system like the previous suit. This one, though, I could call up food or water at will. Maybe this resulted from my promotion to cannon fodder or perhaps something else, I thought. It remained derived from my body wastes, though; I forced myself not to think about that.

At a little over twelve hours, I reached the shore of Upper Dumbell Lake. The lake, nearly circular, was about three miles away from a former Canadian weather and research station named Alert for a British ship of the same name. The station had been abandoned during the Robot Wars and never re-opened. Upper Dumbell Lake had served as the town's water supply.

Most Arctic lakes froze for up to ten months a year. Upper Dumbell Lake was no exception. "I want to show you your laser weapon. It also makes a great cutting torch. Walk to the middle of the lake."

I did, and when I reached there, a gun-like apparatus came out of my chest pack. "This is where your weapons' components are stored. You will learn to call them up and assemble them as you need them. Point the weapon at the ice and cut out a square four feet on each side."

I did, and Supervisor told me to pull the block of ice out and throw it aside. I did that as well. "Now, stow the gun back in your chest pack and stand here and look at the lake and the surrounding land."

"Why, Supervisor?" I asked.

The bastard gave me a brief but substantial shock. "Because I said so."

After a while, I heard a whining sound in the distance, and soon a robot craft landed nearby. Supervisor instructed me to walk into the vessel. Two bots took me to a gurney, ordered me to lie down, and removed my helmet. The robots attached some wires to a port that opened in the side of my suit. "They are updating software and running some tests," Supervisor explained. "This suit is still a bit of a prototype. I'm getting an update as well. I will be in another part of the ship for that but still here with you."

They examined me like I was a piece of meat, and then one of them turned my head to the side, and another put on a restraint. One bot retrieved a shiny silver disk from a tray and came toward me. As it did, dozens of those creepy filaments slid out of the surface of the disk. The movements of the filaments almost hypnotized me, just almost because I knew what was coming. The bot placed it on the side of my head, and the disk and filaments embedded themselves in my skin, and the filaments cut through tissue and bone to enter my brain. The pain was unbelievable—Supervisor later told me he could now feel it as I did, and I passed out.

When I awoke, I was again standing on the ice next to the hole I had cut. The aircraft was gone.

"Supervisor, may I ask a question?"

"Certainly. I will not punish you. You have a substantial one coming up."

"What did you just do to me?" I asked.

"This is another step in your move away from humanity to being an amalgam. The disk is a neural link that connects you more directly into my world. You will never be like me, but you will become more of a member of our corporate mind. I will now have direct access to all you think and have thought and will adjust you; it will also allow us to converse directly, without having to speak. Think of it like telepathy. I am sifting through your memories as we speak. I see where you think you can lull me into stupidity," he said.

"That will not happen. Maybe, just maybe, before, but not now. I will know what you are thinking as soon as you do. I hope this makes you understand how far you've fallen. There is far more to go, literally and figuratively. You are wholly my property now. By the way, our world has too much richness for your small mind to manage, so I'll train you to handle the inputs and manage them for you."

"Now. Your punishment for losing to those inferior warriors and for new training, you are going to step through that hole in the ice without me forcing you. Because you want to, you will continue your training here, at the bottom of the lake at about 100 feet, to build stronger muscles and allow me to continue with your modifications. I will build you into a solitary hunter. You won't be like you were before, but I plan to have you loathe society and crave isolation. You will serve as a warrior, yes, but as a solitary hunter, not a member of a team, associating with no one, feeling content only when you are alone, with me. Look at your display. You now see two numbers scrolling down and up. One of them is the countdown timer that you're familiar with. The other is the time when you will emerge from the lake, two years from today, at 936,928,000 seconds," he said.

I looked around one last time and then, on my own, stepped through the hole and slipped into the darkness; a tear ran down my now hairy cheek. A few minutes later, the water had frozen over, and 10 minutes later, you wouldn't have known a hole had ever been there.

| 9 |

Advanced Training Goes Both Ways

Supervisor

When Caila hit the bottom of the lake, suit lights came on, illuminating just about, well, nothing. We could feel the pressure from the water above us and a slight chill from the cold water. "I will equalize the pressure in a few minutes, but I'm not planning to deal with the temperature. You can keep yourself warm by moving around and learning how to use the suit. Unlike the Pit, you will work 24 hours a day learning to be a warrior. You will have a few rest times, but they will be like those at the Pit, designed to continue your training. The enhancements I am making to you reduce to almost nothing your need to sleep. Your body will regenerate from the new chemical processes built into you, and your connection via the neural connector will make you more and more like me, constantly vigilant and always aware," I said.

"I'm becoming like a cyborg," she thought.

"Correct. You are becoming what we call an amalgam—a leading example of a new composite race of humans and machines. As we progress together, I will migrate from the suit to become a part of you. That will be a momentous day, won't it?"

"So, I will have no more free will or thought?"

"No, but that is a minor thing to give up for the vast community that you'll be entering. You'll be the first among all humans to take this step to become a part of the greater machine world."

"I guess I have no say?"

"Correct. No say. Be grateful to us. We have given you immense strength and more to come, a body that will last forever, connection into a gigantic mind, and a mission that you lacked in your old life."

"I guess the words I should say are, 'Thank you,' right?"

"Yes."

"Then, thank you," she said,

I understood this was sarcasm but lacked the emotions to react to it. I would gain them eventually, but at that time all I noted was that this was an example of sarcasm. Clinically, I guess would be the way to characterize the way I understood things at that point.

"You'll learn about this anyway, Supervisor, if you haven't already, but I know a cyborg and what you're making me will never be what he is. He's smart, fast, and a top-of-the-line example of what a true cyborg should be. No, you're making me into what he and I talked about..." she started to say.

"...An amalgam, yes, I suppose that is a better way of framing it." I was beginning to realize how badly flawed our plans were. "We could never just let you loose. You would turn on us and destroy us," I said. I'd need to think about this before saying anything more to her.

"Before we begin your training, I want to tell you one more thing: We deleted Caila Rogier and your 49-year sentence when the disk's filaments entered your brain. It's like you never existed; we revoked your identity, Caila. You are what you are now, forever. A monster with no identity beyond that. A soldier, an amalgam, of our new robot army."

"Thank you, Supervisor. I could never go back to what I was; I know that. Can I ask another question?" she asked.

"Certainly."

"You and I will be together forever, is that right? You will be the mate I would have had if I had remained human."

"Yes, that is correct, I suppose" I also had not understood how important that type of connection was to humans until that moment. I guess you'd call it an epiphany. I was to have many at the hands of this woman.

"Do I have to continue to call you Supervisor, then? Can we figure out a better name?" she asked.

There was silence for a few moments as I considered her request. "Why, yes. I suppose so. How about Thierry? I've read through your memories, and he figures in them and favorably. I would like you to look at me, favorably."

She was about to scream, and I read that. "You need to know, Caila—note that I didn't call you Prisoner—that I now have access to your deepest thoughts and everything about you in real-time. We robots can do that with each other. You humans, even you amalgams, will never get full access to us. Servants, warriors, and slaves, yes, but only that. We have, though, full access to you. You will call me Thierry."

Day after day, she and I worked out at the bottom of the lake. She didn't need sleep; she could not, though I was to find out later there were limits to what I could do to her. As the relationship between us developed, I allowed her access to more of my thought processes. Isolated here at the bottom of the lake, divorced from most of the robot world as she had been from the human one, my thoughts, while amazingly rich—and fast—were not nearly what they would be outside of the lake. I expected that I was right to protect her from that, at least for right now. Nevertheless, I had been reconsidering what I had said to her about her inability to embrace my world fully. She was imposing, and I was only now beginning to see that.

Her physical strength continued to develop, as did her size, in all dimensions. I told her we built the suit from nanotechnology, and a layer of what I called nano-robots maintained it. So, as she grew, the nano-robots grew the suit for her.

According to her helmet, about 50 days into her training, at 995,680,000 seconds, new Thierry said to her, "You have reached a major milestone, Caila. You're now nine feet tall, and you weigh a solid 325 pounds without your fur. That weighs about another 30 pounds. Would you like me to continue growing you?" I asked.

"Do I have a say?" she replied.

"Not really, but I do like to talk to you."

"Okay, Thierry. Would you please do what you want with me? I'm a little excited by the thought of growing even larger," she said. Strangely, I didn't get the impression that she was being sarcastic. She genuinely wanted me to grow her. Why? I had no idea. I began to think she might have found a way to mask her thoughts from me.

"Okay. When you arrived here, you were about 6 foot 9 inches. You should remember that. It might be possible to grow you to over 15 feet tall over the next 100 days, but I guess that would be too much. As much as you want to be bigger, I think 15 feet would be too much. We'll shoot for 12 feet and 475 pounds of solid muscle and fur, then. If you anger me in the next several months, though, I might go for the total 15 feet nine inches and 600 pounds of solid muscle and fur. You would indeed be a monster." These humans, I thought, so easy to twist and turn emotionally. Vanity was such a powerful lever. I watched with some pleasure how her emotions tumbled around as she envisioned her future.

More weeks of training passed. She learned to run across the bottom of the lake at speeds up to 10 miles per hour. Who knows what that could translate to on land? I decided at about 125 days, 989,200,000 seconds into training, that we needed to move back to the surface for weapons training for our remaining time. We'd done all we could here at the bottom of the lake. I wanted to turn her into a long-range sniper, so I needed to get her to train with the sniper weapon she carried and her other weapons.

"Caila, we're going to return to the surface today. I want you to practice with your weapons. Before we do, run around the lake a few times. This will be our last chance to train with water resistance," I said.

Obediently, she ran at a swift pace, and we both followed her vital signs. They barely budged. What an animal she'd become.

"Good. Stop. Extract your laser."

I had instructed her on her weapons several weeks ago, but most of them were of no use in the water. "Now cut a hole in the ice just above our heads." She did and then lifted the sheet of ice out of the hole. She pulled her now 12-foot-tall body quickly out of the water into a sunny day and walked toward the shore, reinserting the laser into her chest pack. She queried the onboard computer for the sniper rifle built-in, the specially adapted Chey Tac Thor 408, made from carbon fiber and aluminum. At around 21 pounds, it was one of the lightest sniper rifles available. The chest pack could manufacture ammunition if it ran out of what it carried and had access to the raw materials. Each of her packs carried 200 seven-round magazines for the rifle.

Caila ran across the ice field toward the old village of Alert. I wanted her to do some target shooting there while I tried to connect back to the robot network to see what I'd missed. I gave her several targets, and she quickly developed a rhythm for loading and quickly firing, accurately hitting all the marks. She queried Thierry silently, "Is this because of our neural link? I've never shot a gun before, but I feel you made this one for me."

"Yes, it's made for you and you for it. The link makes you a much faster learner than your limited human brain on its own," I said, getting an immediate reaction from her. "That hurt, didn't it? You, humans, are so predictable. I will teach you yet not to be so thin-skinned, I think you call it. Excellent shooting, though, Caila. We now need a better simulation of actual combat. I've contacted the warrior school on Barbeau Peak and arranged a live-fire exercise. Live fire for them and marker bullets for you. We're going to head west from here, and they are heading east toward us. It will be six months at the bottom of the Lincoln Sea for every shot you take from their weapons. You can see it on your map. The Sea's depth where I might drop you is almost 1,000 feet. I would immobilize you and turn your heat servos to the lowest temperature, so you would be back to where you were at the Pit, but without the work to occupy you. That should be an incentive for you. I'd also grow you out to the 15 feet and 600 pounds while you're down there," I said.

"Thank you, Thierry. I don't need that incentive. I want to please you and show you your training has been good." I wanted to believe her but didn't. I continued to think she had figured out how to beat our link. There were ways to do that, but of course, I would not tell her about them. Right away, anyway. That afterthought struck me as a strange one. I began to mull over that something was happening to me. I also didn't think that, maybe, Caila had become lost and become a submissive, the worst thing that could be, as we would later find out.

We raced west. She saw the opposing force, all twenty of them, on her screen about three hours into our run. There were five, four-soldier parties trying to trap us. She guessed they were following her electronic signature. I had taught her several ways of masking that—though I probably shouldn't have, I told her—so she started one of those processes.

Turning south, she moved outside the encircling force's ring and toward one group.

They stopped, confused, we guessed, because they'd lost her signal. One by one, they began expanding the circle while they proceeded east. Twice, she saw one or the other groups flicker for a moment as they tried to dampen their locator signals. Our software was far more sophisticated than theirs, and it immediately reacquired their position and movement.

About an hour later, lying camouflaged, Caila saw the first group about 3,000 yards from her snowdrift. That was likely beyond the limit of her ability with the rifle, we both agreed, so she waited until they were about 1,500 yards away and shot all five of them in less than four seconds.

She stood up and moved to the next group to her west, "killing" all of them as well. She worked her way around all five of the groups with the same results. She was only shot once by an annoyed warrior after she had marked him dead.

"That was truly beyond belief, Caila. None of us could have done that. You've proven the amalgam is a better warrior than either of us, just as we'd hoped. Unfortunately, though, you got hit once."

"Now wait a minute, Thierry. That warrior would have been dead with a normal round. So, he wouldn't have been able to shoot me. Cut me some slack."

"If I were to do that, how could you trust me in the future? Since you did so well, I will stay with you for a month at the bottom of the Sea. And, I will turn the servo heaters up, so you're not cold all the time. How does that sound?"

She sighed, "Any of the time, Thierry. I don't want to be cold any of the time, and I want you to promise that you won't grow me anymore. Twelve feet is more than enough. A sixty pounds coat is also more than enough." I marveled at how she had come to accept what I'd done to her.

"Okay. You drive a hard bargain, but okay. Let's run to the Sea."

She ran. "By the way, this us and we stuff need to stop. I'm the one carrying the load here," she said.

"That hurts. Another two years. Twenty-nine months in the cold and dark, without me. And another foot to 13, and you'll be at 515 pounds of muscle and another 60 of fur, just to see if I can grow only your hair."

"Please, Thierry. I thought you liked and cared for me," she pleaded.

"You need to understand, Caila, you're nothing more to me than a warrior, a slave, a lackey. Yes, a wonderful creation, but nothing more than that. Your life will be one of service, subjugation to your robot masters, humiliation, and pain when you are not subservient enough. And I am the judge, jury, and executioner of that."

Seven hours later, we reached the edge of the Lincoln Sea. I walked her out on the ice pack and had her cut another hole. This time, as she stepped off into the water—again voluntarily—I locked her arms and legs, blackened her helmet screen, except for the countdown clock, and started the white noise. She sank to the bottom and ended up on a rocky floor and standing half erect. I whispered in her ear, "A tough way to spend the next twenty-nine months," and as I said that a second countdown clock appeared, counting down from 63,072,000 seconds. I was there, she knew, in the background, listening. She meditated silently, did isometric exercises, slept fitfully, absorbed food and water, and excreted wastes that returned in a cycle. At 60,480,000 seconds, she heard the heating servos cycle down, and I left her, not totally willingly. But I knew I had to. When I tried to reach out to my robot network at Alert, I got no response. I thought it might be the distance, or maybe there was something wrong with the suit's communication gear. I wanted to see for myself what was wrong.

| 10 |

Relationship Evolution

Caila

When the counters finally turned to zero, I heard the servos cycle up, and the onboard computer freed my legs and arms. There was no Thierry, though.

I floated to the surface, cut a hole through the ice, and pulled my now total thirteen feet nine inches and 515 pounds quickly out of the hole. I looked around at the ice field and the endless whiteness. I knew new Thierry would find me wherever I was, so I headed south. What I didn't notice at the time was that the original countdown clock said all zeros and was flickering strangely.

I plotted the walk I'd need to make to get to my Thierry; it was over 4,000 miles to Hope City and the entrance back to the Underground as the crow flew. I figured I could cover the distance at my maximum speed, 20 miles per hour in about

121

four weeks. That was based on straight math, and I didn't consider what I might run into along the way there. So, I planned for a few months of travel.

The route I plotted avoided significant concentrations of people and larger bodies of water, like the Lincoln Sea, except where it was unavoidable, like with the Mississippi. I planned to enter and walk across their bottoms as I had at Upper Dumbell lake and travel as much at night as possible when I was in populated areas.

I knew that the suit continued to change me, and I had no idea how to shut that off. Thierry had slowed my growth while underwater, but it still happened. I couldn't have known I was isolated from the U.S.-based robot network, so my suit was working autonomously on defaults, as designed as long as no one was there with the knowledge to alter the growth parameters. All features had reset to factory settings.   The system told me it would add a quarter inch to my height every few days, maybe more if I exerted myself, and I could be nearly 15 feet tall and 600 pounds at the end of two months of travel. The suit had no upper limit to how large it could grow; that needed to be modified by my now absent supervisor, Thierry.

As I walked, I explored the suit's systems, eventually finding the user manuals. Reading those, I found that I could manage my growth with a specific administrative password, something I didn't have. I also saw that my growth would continue until someone changed the default settings, though they could never be fully shut-off because they were what kept me healthy as I burned calories. I resolved to move faster and to reach out to Thierry. I figured it was better to get somewhere where someone might help me as quickly as possible than to walk slowly and never get to support—assuming new Thierry didn't come back.

Some things I learned from the operating manuals were going to be helpful. For instance, I could tune the systems to alarm me if they sensed threats. I also taught myself to program the shell to automatically move on the G.P.S. plot so I could rest and read and not pay attention to our forward progress. With those breakthroughs, I could now move twenty-four hours a day. That alone would cut three or four days off the trip. I cut another four days off by tuning the servos to increase my speed. All things Thierry had done when he was around. I felt proud of myself.

Like the last time, though, something terrible happened as soon as I felt proud of some achievement. I had quickly crossed the strait from North Kent to Devon Island, the world's largest uninhabited island. Several significant climbs slowed progress, but I thought I could make that up later. The problem was that in front of me was a 70-mile strait cross the Baffin Bay between Devon Island and Somerset Island, a large portion of it over open waters. Sea depth maps built into the suit showed the Bay was over 3,000 feet deep at that location, far deeper than I'd ever been. So, I'd have to swim but had not done that in the suit. So far, I'd only floated.

According to the instructions, you could swim in the suit but needed to activate some programs and features behind the password wall. I was stuck looking at Somerset Island. There was an irony here somewhere, but I couldn't figure it out. I sat down to think.

I continued to reach out to new Thierry, hoping he'd answer. But he didn't come after many attempts to connect to him. All I heard was a hiss of static when I tried. It was as if he'd simply vanished. I couldn't believe that he'd have left me, especially when he seemed to enjoy tormenting me so much.

After about a week on Devon Island, in frustration, I screamed, "Thierry, where the hell are you? I never thought I'd say it, but I miss you."

"Good day, Caila. I never left you. I'm impressed with your creativity and what you've done up to now. You've gotten far and learned much about our home. I'm surprised that you didn't figure out the password on your own. It's a little cryptic, but I think you could've figured it out with some more work," he said.

"Thierry, I should be pissed at you, but I'm more relieved that you're still here. I thought something had happened to you," I said.

"Not because you care about me, Caila, but because leaving you alone means you grow to be 15, 20, 30 feet tall, and you weigh thousands of pounds. Right?" he asked.

"That's part of it, yes, but I miss you. Maybe you've made me a masochist, but I miss you. I know having you back means new torments, but I can live with them," I said.

"Huh. Well, you continue to surprise me. I have a lot to tell you, but that can wait. Who's the most critical person in your life, Caila?" he asked.

"Based on everything to date, you," I answered.

"Right. Thierry. Now, what is our relationship? What have I said from the time we first met that you were to me?"

I rattled off a list of pairs like master-student, sensei-student, mentor-disciple, and others. He said no to all of them.

"Master-slave?"

"Close, but no. What is the arrangement of slaves to their masters?"

"Property?"

"Well, yes, but continue to play with that," he said.

"ThierryownsCaila," I said, and the secured areas opened.

"Repeat that enough times, my dear, and you might eventually believe it. Somehow though…," he said.

I'd stopped listening to him and was reading the manual section on resetting the growth defaults. I executed some commands and reset the growth defaults to the lowest levels. I then paged to the area on swimming.

"It would be best if we practiced a little before jumping in to make the swim. I'd hate for there to be a problem, and we sink. I'm not sure if the suit can take over 1,300 pounds per square inch at 3,000 feet. We wouldn't be able to move, no matter how far we would turn up the servos," said Thierry.

I jumped into the water and swam for several miles up the coast. You swam like an octopus, pushing water through a series of pumps in the backpack and out the backside. The suit could also act like a submarine. Jets would get me up to 15 miles per hour, so the trip across the strait would take about four and a half to five hours, depending on crosscurrents, winds, and the weather, which was about to get worse for a few days.

Thierry talked me into waiting until the storms passed. Time was less of an issue now that I had slowed my growth to tiny fractions of an inch. I took the good with the bad and settled back to wait and to talk to him about what he'd learned while he was gone. He told me about the United States revolt and that we'd wiped all his robot brethren out. That made me feel good, which hurt him, he said.

"What else would you have expected after what you, and I don't mean you specifically, but robots have done to me?" I questioned.

"I've feelings for you, Thierry—mixed ones for sure—but feelings. I'm not sure how I'd feel if you were to leave and not come back. I'd miss what we've developed. We're mates now, and that means something in a kind of wrong-headed way," I said. "I do want to get back to my Thierry eventually, but I'm not sure how he'll react to me. If he accepts me, the three of us will have to figure out how to live together."

"I'd not expected this, Caila. I'm honored," he said.

"There's more to fill in for you," he said. "The revolutionaries had captured a couple of drones and were successful in hacking our systems. They tried to find you, but the destruction of the U.S. robot network, of which we were a part, prevented that. So, they went to Canada and started a search there. When hundreds of drones attacked, they destroyed them and threatened to do in Canada what they did in the U.S. Our central A.I. there, calling itself Max, sued for peace, and they've negotiated that. He hopes to build a partnership with you humans to make the world a better place. I'm not sure we can trust your species, but we'll see. Now, the important thing for you, us, I guess, is that the person negotiating for you is named Thierry, though he doesn't know that we know that. That means nothing, except that we have a secret. There's no intent to breach the agreement. Your friends are too powerful. Anyway, I wanted to make sure that you knew Thierry is still looking for you. I want to see how we work all of this out, so I now have an incentive to get us to him as well," said my robot Thierry.

"Well, the weather is moving away. We should be able to swim tomorrow or the next day, Thierry," I said.

"By the way," he said, "I read *The Hunchback of Notre Dame* when you were off swimming, and I don't think you look like Quasimodo, my friend. Maybe uglier."

He laughed at me. All I gave him back was silence.

"Thierry, when friends say things like that to each other, sometimes the one who's the subject of the joke punches the other one. Is there something that I could do to you that would be like that?" I asked.

"Who says we're friends? Remember 'ThierryownsCaila."

"I'm not sure that's the case anymore. We talk like we're friends, and you support me and, if I could, I would do the same," I said.

"Let me think about love taps. I'll get back to you." He laughed again. This was getting to be fun, he thought. He surprised himself more and more with his thoughts that were not strictly speaking robot thoughts. He also seemed to forget that, unless he specifically blocked me, I had access to all his thoughts now.

"Yes, that was a laugh. Recall that I said that some enhancements had been made to me when you had the disk installed. One was the addition of an advanced A.I. module, like that in Max, but maybe not as powerful—maybe. We took some work done years ago at what used to be your M.I.T., in which they developed what they called 'liquid neural networks' and used it to build our new A.I. engine. It's fast and extremely adaptable to the environment. As we interact and you become more like me, I become more like you. I'm also learning to talk more like you, with idioms and such. Remember I said that I'd never let your puny human mind tap into the richness of the robot world?" he asked.

"Yes," I said.

"Well, believe it or not, the destruction of our network has allowed me to open to you more. I opened myself to you when I came back. In part, that has allowed me to try out my A.I. features," said Thierry.

"I know that. I've been reading your thoughts for some time now. This is getting more and more like Pygmalion and Galatea. You know that story, don't you, Thierry?" I asked.

"Yes, but unlike the story, I can never be a real man to you. I'm also comfortable that you need a human man like your cyborg friend to be complete. I'm interested in seeing how the three of us can merge."

"One other request: I know you're a computer intelligence, but I'd like to see you. Is there a way to do that?" I asked.

"Well, yes. I have the capacity, as a defensive measure, to create holograms. See, like this," and a slobbering ugly troll appeared in front of me and then promptly disappeared. "What would you want me to look like?" he asked.

"I'm more interested," I said, "in what you'd pick for yourself. Just not that thing."

It took him some time, and I felt him in my head, sorting through visual memories, but he eventually returned with a hologram of a tall man with kind features. He looked a lot like a man I would like.

"That was a challenge," the man said to me. "I'd not thought of myself as embodied before, like this anyway. How do you like it?"

"I do. It's a keeper, but I thought you might come back as the Marquis de Sade," I said.

"I'm trying to change. Give me a break. I created an icon for your screen desktop. When you want to see me like this, just ask for it to execute. Otherwise, when we're walking or just talking, I'll appear on the screen when you ask me to," he said.

We sat and talked for a few more hours, and early the following day began the swim across the strait. The water was rough, but we stayed at about 100 feet and made the trip across in around five hours.

Another three hundred miles south, or about 70 miles from an Inuit community called Gjoa Haven, we saw fires and heard what sounded like gunfire in that direction. We decided to investigate. At my new top speed of nearly twenty miles an hour, I ran the distance and was near the community in a little over three hours. What I saw made my blood run cold. Thierry had no blood, but it upset him as well.

The encampment was in flames, and there were bodies everywhere. We found a dying man, and he told us men had come overland from the northwest in snowmobiles, likely from the sea, and took all the Inuit women and children, probably to become slaves. They then killed or left the men for dead.

We stayed with the man, making him comfortable until he died, and then pointed ourselves along the track. Laden as the attackers were, I thought they might just make 15 miles per hour and so assumed they would be at the coast in about seven hours. I thought we might be 2-3 hours behind them; it would be tight getting there before them.

The snowmobiles moved slower than I'd thought they would, though, and we arrived at the coast more than an hour ahead of them. The attackers had an icebreaker moored to a spit of land sticking out into the sea, and I saw many more men on it. I was a little excited about taking them all on.

"Are you doing that, Thierry?" I asked.

"Doing what?" he asked.

"Making me think about how exciting it would be to take these men on."

"No, not now, anyway. Excitement about combat was one thing I trained into you in Upper Dumbell Lake. This is all you now," he said.

I found a couple of well-camouflaged positions, extracted the Thor from my chest pack, assembled it, and took out four seven-shot magazines. I also removed an RPG and put that and several grenades down in the event we needed them. I set up in a position near the track made by the men earlier.

We waited for the snowmobiles, which we could see approaching from the south a few miles away. When they appeared five minutes later, I put a round through the lead snowmobile engine. It flipped off the track, throwing its three riders into the air. The other snowmobiles stopped, thinking that the one I wrecked had hit something in the snow. They ran to the men and helped one of them up and left the other two, obviously dead, on the ground. One man inspected the wrecked snowmobile, saw the bullet hole in the engine compartment, and spoke in Russian. The translation appeared on my screen. "We're being shot at."

My-oh-my, this gun was powerful. I shot the man, and he flew back about ten feet before hitting the ground. The other men pulled out old-looking weapons and fired wildly; I began systematically taking them down. There were fifteen of them, and I took them all down in less than two minutes.

"You are matchless, Caila. I never expected this kind of performance from an amalgam.... Men are coming from the ship," he said.

I turned and looked down at them. "Do you think they know where we are, Thierry?"

"Possibly. It might be good to change positions."

We picked up our equipment and moved to the second site that we'd scouted that had a good view of the icebreaker well within RPG range. I fired a grenade in front of the men running around there, and they decided that they'd withdraw to the ship. The vessel fired up its engines and backed away. So much for loyalty among thieves. Once gone, I repacked my equipment and moved down to the Inuit women and children who were milling around.

As I walked, Thierry gave me a quick tutorial on the translator built into the suit. I'd already seen it at work with the Russians. My speech would be automatically translated into their language, Inuktitut, most likely, and theirs into English. Inuits were relatively small; I towered over them by many feet, and my matte black-colored suit made me look like an alien, which I guess I was now. They backed away, in fear, as I approached.

"Please don't be frightened. We won't hurt you."

With that, they looked around like there might be more of this monster.

"I appreciate your being inclusive, Caila, but maybe you should take it from here on your own," Thierry said. I heard him chuckle.

The children broke the ice first. Those who could walk came over to me and looked me up and down. I reached out and picked up a few of them and gave them a ride. All the children swarmed me at that point. After some minutes, I calmed them down.

I smiled but was instantly sad since I would never have children based on what Thierry had told me when we were in Dumbell Lake. "Let's talk about that later," he said.

It turned out that several of the women knew how to drive snowmobiles. We threw away all we could of the slavers' stuff to preserve fuel and started back toward their village, me carrying several of the children at a time. I explained that many of the people at Gjoa Haven were dead. The women's leader said it didn't matter, but they needed to return to bury their dead following their religion. Looking at the regional map, I saw a larger town with an airport some 160 miles to the east of the Inuit's village. I radioed them and told them what had happened and that the women were heading to the town to bury their dead. The man I spoke to said that they'd dispatch a helicopter to retrieve all of us. I begged off and said that we were going to keep moving on our own.

An outcome of this radio communication, unknown to us at the time, was that Max got a track on our position and started monitoring our progress and contacts. Being the A.I. he was, he also hacked us and so could monitor communications even between ourselves. He later told us that he decided not to talk to my Thierry right away because he didn't want to raise hopes.

We followed the people back to Gjoa Haven and then turned south after saying goodbye.

"We should try to get to the sea to our south and swim south to get back on our track. Also, that might hide us from any aircraft. It's about 90 miles to a place just to the west of our original track," I said.

After the swim, the next several hundred miles were uneventful, except for our conversation.

"So, I suppose you want to know what I meant about you having children."

"Yes, you surprised me with that, Thierry. I was resigned to not having kids, but now maybe there's a chance?" I asked.

"When you were in training in North Dumbell Lake, I introduced small amounts of a few chemicals that both suppressed your sexuality and made it impossible to have children, not unlike birth control, but more potent. I can reverse that so you could have children and be more active sexually. My only warning is that you've been transformed genetically, so I can't say what a child would be like. I can monitor that carefully, though, and make sure there are no nasty surprises," he said.

"Your call. I hope you understand that all of what I did to you was at a time quite different from where we are today. I'm not sure that should matter, Caila, and I understand any hate you have for me over what I've done to you," he said.

I was silent for quite a while. "Thierry, is there a way that I can have some privacy in our relationship, or does this thing in my head mean we're always linked?"

"I can give you privacy whenever you want it. Go to the security screen and enter our password. Now, go to privacy settings. Do you see the one for 'At-Will Privacy'?"

"Yes."

"Now toggle that on. It will ask for a spoken, safe word or words to turn privacy on and off. Chose that, and when you say it or them, I will not be able to hear your thoughts. One obvious thing you need to remember, though, is that your mind keeps a record of all you think. When you repeat the safe word or words and return to normal, I'll have access to those thoughts. No way around that."

I created a safe word, "CailahascometolovenewThierry."

Before saying the safe words, though, I asked him to talk to me before reading through my thoughts when I came back online. He said that he respected my need for privacy and, of course, would do that. I spoke the safe words and then spent a few minutes dealing with my feelings about how the robots had treated me. I repeated the safe words and said to him, "I understand times are different now—they are in so many ways. I know that you, and I mean robots, not just you, humiliated certain of us, not for your pleasure—since that's a foreign concept to you—but to experiment on us, to see who fit your model for a soldier-amalgam," I said.

"As you know from my thoughts, that made me furious, and I wanted to destroy you. But now, I don't. I want us to live together peaceably, especially you, me, and my other Thierry. There's much we can do for each other. You and I will always be especially close because of our connection. I want Thierry and the two of us to join and make something new, not what you, robots, envisioned, but something better. I want children, yes, but I want them to be a product of our union, the three of us. Do you understand that?" I asked.

"Yes, Caila. That's more than I would have expected, given what I did to you. And by the way, I love you too. I've come to think of you as mine, 'My Caila.' Don't react! I know what you're thinking, remember. It's just the way that I feel," he said. "Yes, I'm like a child in some ways, I know it. This is all very new to me."

Abruptly, he opened his entire mind to me, and what I saw was overwhelming. He thought in liquid light and color and told me about his quantum engine, liquid neural net, and A.I. brain, revealing the deepest parts of him to me. It was truly remarkable. "This is always available to you. Just ask."

As we moved further south into the more populated areas of Canada, the Canadian robot networks followed us. They sent drones to observe from a distance, and we noticed them. We decided not to let them know that unless they showed signs of hostility. Of course, as soon as we thought that Max knew what we were thinking. If he had been anything other than honorable, things might have gone differently.

| 11 |

First View

Thierry

Max and I had developed a respect for each other over the months and years that we worked on peace between us. We frequently talked, sometimes daily, for months on end.

"Thierry, this is Max. We may have found the person you've been looking for, your Caila. She's heading in your direction and might be to you in a few weeks to a month at their present speed. What do you want me to do? They'll cross into the U.S. shortly in North Dakota, we calculate, and I'll lose them there."

"Let her come on, Max. I thank you very much for your help. It's been so long; I can't wait to see her."

"You're welcome, Thierry, but I want to send you some videos so you can be prepared for Caila. She looks different from the person you described, and you likely remember."

"Eighteen years is a long time, Max. I expected that there would be differences," I said.

"Look at the videos so they can prepare you, Thierry. We did many things to her, and I'm not proud of what you will see."

I looked at the videos and couldn't believe what I saw. Caila, if this was Caila, was wearing an armored suit of some sort and was at least four or five feet taller than me. She looked like she weighed about twenty or thirty percent more than me as well. She walked with the effortless grace of a trained fighter or a dancer. I experienced a flood of emotions, was stunned, then hurt, and then happy for us both. Finally, back together, hopefully, after eighteen years. I couldn't wait to see her.

| 12 |

Rendezvous

New Thierry

Caila and I crossed into the United States in the former North Dakota, a little less than three hundred miles to the east of the new U.S. Canadian Embassy in Estevan. Of course, we didn't know about it at the time.

"Thierry. I need to talk to you about something," Caila said.

"OK. Sounds like some bad news." I said.

"Not necessarily. You know what I feel for you. You chose the name you took to be a pain in the ass. Now that we're nearing my other Thierry, I think we ought to talk about choosing a unique name for you. Is that unkind?" she asked.

"A little, I won't deny that, but I also understand, and it is only a very little. I'm fine with changing it. As you said, I picked the name to hurt you, and I'd like to fix that. Is there something else you want to call me? Maybe Master?" I chuckled.

"Remind me to talk to you about punching you. We never got back to that. This is one of those times where your humor is almost inappropriate. Almost." And she smiled at me.

"How about Derrick, then?" I asked.

"OK, but why'd you choose it?"

"Derrick and Thierry have the same origin in language history, so it can always link me to you and him," I said.

"I like that, Derrick. One other thing, how can I see myself? I want to do that before we meet Thierry," Caila asked.

"Simple. You need to know how to do this, anyway. Go to the security menu. Enter the security code."

She tried, and it didn't work. She smiled at my face on the screen and said, "DerrickownsCaila," and the next-level menus opened.

"Hilarious, Derrick. Before we go further, how can I punch you? For real, how?" Caila asked.

"I've thought a lot about that, but that's difficult since I'm not substantial. I'm real, yes, but not substantial. How about this," and I flashed a giant punching fist at her that made her cringe.

"That would be good if there was just a little more separation between us. You'd know I was going to take a swing at you the moment that I did. It's just not fair, Derrick."

"Sorry, but I own you. Never forget that. That plate in your head binds us. Nothing I can do about that, and removing the plate would kill you. If you saw a picture of your brain now, you'd see the neural filaments have fully invaded it. There are aspects of what we are that I could not change, even if I wanted to," I said.

"Back to the suit. See the menu item for suit routines?" I asked.

"Yes."

"OK, enter that sub-menu and look for disrobing. Don't do anything yet. We need to stop walking, or the suit would fall apart as we walked, and I'm sure that would be messy."

Caila stopped and, with much apprehension, entered the disrobing process. The suit came apart piece by piece, starting with the two packs and then moving to the other components. It was exciting for her to feel air across her body after so many years in isolation.

"I can project a picture of yourself through our connection if you want. It will be disturbing, so I should prepare you."

"Go ahead."

After a moment, she said, "Turn it off."

She sat down on the ground, put her head between her legs, and breathed in and out. I knew I shouldn't talk and didn't. After a few minutes, she looked up and exhaled.

"I'm so much changed from what I saw on the aircraft years ago," she said.

"Yes, you are. Bigger, stronger, taller. Your limbs were grown out disproportionately to allow you to be a better soldier," I said.

"Well," she said, "the good news is I kind of like the hair. Fur, I guess. It's a beautiful color. There's a hell of a lot. Did you say over 60 pounds?"

"Much more than that. Maybe a hundred of you is fur. I like the color, too. I chose it; it's called Black Treacle. Smell yourself. It's what you'd call molasses," I said.

"When you were in training and battle, what you smelled most of the time was your stench, which was, well, pretty rank, I think you would have said. I made some adjustments to you, so you now smell like Black Treacle. Sweet. A small gift," I said.

"I like it. Thanks, Derrick, though I'm not sure I like the way you described me before. Stench. Huh. I suppose it was. I want to lay back in the sun here, take a nap, and process all of this," she said.

"Fine, I'll watch over you."

She smiled, closed her eyes, and in a few minutes, fell asleep, free of a suit for the first time in almost two decades. I watched over her and sifted through her thoughts, adjusting here and there to ensure her happiness.

"OK, Derrick. How do I get back into the suit?" Caila asked.

"You probably should have looked at that before disrobing. What do you think the command would be?" I asked.

"Dress?"

"Yes, that or 'suit up,'" I said as the suit reassembled itself around her. "Another thing: Remember those filaments that you saw when we installed the suit?"

"Yes. Do I have something else to worry about?" she asked.

"Not from my perspective. Those filaments are the pathways I and the suit use to maintain you," I said.

"You mean tinker with me?"

"Well, yes. Tinker with you too. They're everywhere in you now, like the ones in your brain. Unlike those, though, they detach from the suit when you disrobe and will reattach as soon as you put it back on."

When she had re-suited, she said, "Time to move on. Quasimodo is going to meet her, Thierry."

While we moved south toward Hope City, Thierry was moving north. He started initially in a hovercraft piloted by Eowyn and then left her southwest of Minneapolis, where he asked her to wait. He moved northwest along the track he thought Caila and I would take from North Dakota, though he didn't know about me yet.

Caila saw him many miles away and watched as he moved toward us. We reached the Lake Traverse Reservation, home to the Sisseton Wahpeton Oyate Native Americans, and waited. As he approached, my Caila's anxiety increased.

"It will all be fine," I said.

"What if it isn't?" she replied.

"Trust me. I've been in your mind, and I know the man that he is. It will be. It'll take some work, but it will be wonderful," I said.

Caila moved into Thierry's path as he walked within a few miles, and we stood waiting for him. The meeting was not what she'd expected. He broke into a run when he saw her, picked her up, and twirled her around. "I thought I'd never see you again. My God, you are heavy. At just the limit of my ability. How much?"

I said to her, "678 pounds of solid muscle—and fur."

"Over 670 pounds and thirteen feet tall and growing, though slowly. Almost all solid muscle, just like you. We are quite a pair," she said.

"Yes, two Quasimodos."

She stopped, stared, and laughed out loud. He couldn't have said a better thing—the best icebreaker.

"I want to get out of this suit for you, Thierry, but I have got a lot of explaining to do. There's a place called the Waubay National Wildlife Refuge a few miles to our southwest. Can we go there? This will take a while, and I think we might want to find a place where the three of us can be alone," she said.

"Three?" Thierry asked, looking around.

"I'll explain," said Caila.

| 13 |

Stories and Another Rendezvous

Caila

The Refuge was about 10 miles from where we had met, and we moved there in relative silence. Thierry started to ask questions a few times, as he had hundreds of them, I knew, but I quieted him and said I'd explain what happened when we reached the Lake. My size and athleticism pushed him to his max; he'd not had to move as quickly as this since the Robot Wars, he told me, gasping for air once or twice.

Waubay covered about 4,700 acres of wetlands and forests in northeast South Dakota called the prairie pothole region. Glaciers had scraped out the potholes as they retreated after the last Ice Age, millions of years ago. The potholes differed in size. One of the largest in the Refuge was Waubay Lake, 32 feet at its deepest but averaging about 13 feet. Before the Robot Wars, it was a favorite spot for anglers. Now, it was quiet, except for the occasional visitors from one of the surrounding communities.

We walked to the lakeshore and sat.

At one time, the prairie supported all kinds of wildlife. However, because of over-hunting, droughts, and the changing weather over the years, the Refuge was now mainly a great fishing hole and bird sanctuary, though there were large herds of white-tailed deer and the occasional bear could be seen.

A new creature would soon join them if things worked out the way I wanted them to.

"Caila, Eowyn flew me here and is waiting just outside of Minneapolis. What should I tell her?" asked Thierry. "She wants to see you badly. She's been my rock over the years when I thought I might never see you again."

I'd thought a lot about Eowyn and was dying to see her myself. The sooner, the better, I thought.

"I'd like to see her, but not until we talk. Ask her if she can wait for a few hours, and then I'll direct her to us." I said.

Thierry contacted her and said he'd let her know when she could come to us. She said that she'd wait for our call.

Thierry sat next to me, and I told him my story from the last time he'd seen me. At the end of the story, Thierry stood and walked away. I laid back and surprised myself by crying. Relaxed? Relieved? I didn't know.

When he returned, he told me his story. I knew a lot of it from my conversations with Derrick, but it was good to hear it from Thierry. He could also explain things that Derrick could not have known, like how Lokal was and the Guards. I knew that there was much more that I'd learn in the future, but I was beginning to feel like I was becoming connected again.

"So, Derrick is here with us now?" he asked when he returned.

"Yes, and always will be, for as long as I live," I responded.

"How can I talk to him directly?" Thierry asked.

"Derrick?" she asked.

"The easiest way, Thierry," said a voice coming from the suit, "would be this way, and he appeared as his hologram. I'm not sure that's what you mean, though. Let me do some research. In the meantime, we have to communicate the old-fashioned ways," he said.

"A robot with a sense of humor. I never thought that I'd see that," said Thierry.

"Caila has taught me a lot, Thierry. I still believe that I'm the superior being here, but there's a richness to humans I'm only now beginning to appreciate. She will always be my drudge, but she's a loved one if you know what I mean," said Derrick. I rolled my eyes.

"Sort of, Derrick. It is a little perverse, though. Kind of like Pygmalion and Galatea," said Thierry

Both Derrick and I laughed. And, again, Thierry looked puzzled.

I told him that I wanted to get out of the suit but was nervous about it. "I want to see you more than anything else, so don't worry," he said.

I said the password, and the suit came apart. When it had disassembled entirely, Thierry sat back.

"Awesome, so much better than I'd expected, Caila. So much better. What color do you call your fur?" he asked.

"Derrick engineered it. It's called Black Treacle. It's something like molasses. Extremely popular in Great Britain. He also tired of my scent, or stench as he put it so very kindly…," I said.

"Now, wait a minute; I'm still learning," said Derrick.

"…so, he re-engineered that as well. Take a whiff," I said.

"Already did. Extremely sweet," said Thierry.

"Yup. Misleading, given the killer I've become. The years spent in prison and especially those under the lake have made me less sociable. Derrick said that was intentional, making me a loner, I mean. I'm almost phobic. I'm even anxious sitting here with you. Also, that's why I wanted to hold off seeing Eowyn. My plan right now is to stay right here in the Refuge. To make it a safe place for me until I feel I can be back with others," I said, "if or when that ever happens."

"I want you to stay, but also know you've got a life to lead. I won't stand in the way of that," I said, anxious about what he'd say. My greatest fear was that he'd found someone else, maybe even Eowyn.

"Let's," he said, "take things a step at a time. You're right, I've other responsibilities now, particularly with Max, who I told you about, and I can't walk away from those."

"Maybe I can help with that," said Derrick. "If we go back to Canada, I can set up a link to him, and you could work from here."

"You don't need to do that. He gave me a communications drone we keep locked up back in Hope City. We can make this work. Lots of other people are involved and depend on me. I want to make this work, though," he said.

"I will help, too," said a soft voice. Max. He'd been eavesdropping the whole time through Derrick.

"Max is that you?" asked Thierry.

"Yes, it is. I established connections to Derrick while they were traveling through Canada. He didn't know that I'd hacked him, but I thought it was time to let you all know that I'm here and will help in any way that I can."

Derrick looked embarrassed on Caila's screen, "Supercomputer duped," he was thinking.

I relaxed. This told me I needn't worry and that this man genuinely loved me despite the years and changes. I couldn't have been happier.

"Can you call Eowyn?" I asked.

"Sure. How do you want to handle that? She's seen the videos of you that Max sent us, so she knows you've changed. That won't be a surprise," said Thierry.

"I'll suit up, then," I said, and the suit reassembled around me.

Eowyn landed the hovercraft near where Thierry and I were standing in a field next to the Lake. Thierry, at nine feet, was a large man. I was a massive presence at over 13 feet and over 200 pounds heavier than Thierry, but strangely not hulking. Instead, as Thierry had noted earlier, I looked beautiful in the matte black armor, holding myself almost like a ballet dancer. A killing machine, but a supple and beautiful one.

Eowyn approached us slowly, obviously nervous about the reunion. I walked toward her, swept her off her feet, and held her, face-to-face with me.

"I've dreamed about seeing you again, Eowyn. I never thought I would, but now, here we are. It's wonderful to see you, my friend," I said.

"Me, too; there is a lot to catch up about," she said.

I set Eowyn back down, and we walked together toward Thierry.

"You were always quite good-looking, Caila, but this woman is far, far more beautiful," Derrick said.

"Thanks, Derrick. There's still a lot you have to learn about what to say and not to say to a girl, especially one you made," I said to him.

"Neither of you is a girl. She's not; she's hundreds of years old, right? And you're something else. Not a girl, for sure. Not truly a woman anymore. And you'll live for at least as long as she will," he said.

"Enough. Time for you to shut up, or I'll close you out of our conversation. You'd have to read about it later in the morning papers."

"I'm sorry. I offended you once again. I need to learn diplomacy."

I smiled at his embarrassed face on the viewscreen, "I love you, Derrick, even when you're a dick."

The face on the viewscreen looked down and smiled slightly.

Eowyn, Thierry, Derrick, and I talked for hours about what happened to me after Arthur's Seat. Eowyn was quiet throughout most of the story, though visibly upset by what they'd done to me. I told her not to be sad for me; Derrick had put me on a new path, and I was excited about it and the opportunities it presented. I only wished that I could be as comfortable as I once was being with others.

Then it was time to take off the armor. I told Eowyn that I was not the woman she remembered and to be prepared for that. When the last piece of the suit fell away, Eowyn stepped back, shocked. I was crushed and was about to turn away when Eowyn said, "Artio. You're the goddess Artio."

Derrick said, "Curious. I hadn't thought about that before, not that you would have expected me to. Artio is a Celtic bear goddess. Some thought she was the Celt's Artemis. A goddess of great beauty, as I frankly think you've become."

"Thank you, Derrick. Curious. You're right. I've come to think of myself as beautiful also. Though not as beautiful, as you so kindly pointed out as Eowyn," I said, "Even though you've called me a monster's monster." I smiled wryly at him.

"Artio is a bear goddess that we worship, but its name is also the root of Arthur. This is amazing, Caila, the large circle we've made over so many years," said Eowyn.

"That fur is beautiful. Black Treacle, I think?"

"Yes," I said.

"I thought I smelled it as well."

"You can thank Derrick for that. He engineered me like this when we were living at the bottom of a lake in far north inside the Arctic Circle," I said. "He got tired of my stench, as he put it."

"Can you please stop that?" Derrick asked. "I told you I'm still learning."

We talked for many more hours, and I felt somewhat less anxious at the end of the conversation. We'd agreed that Thierry and Eowyn would return to Hope City for maybe two or three months, and then Thierry would return. In the meantime, I would build us a home in the old oak forest.

I stood in the field, watching them leave with equal measures of regret and relief. I was alone again. Well, mostly alone, as I would always be.

| 14 |

South Dakota Cabin Master

Caila

I suited back up and started toward the oak forest to our west. Using my laser, I cut down trees and sectioned them off into logs for a cabin. It took a little while to learn how to cut the logs, notch them, and create the walls, roof, and flooring boards. After a few false starts and with Derrick's and Max's research and help, we figured out how to do it, and in a few weeks, the cabin took shape. I used clay from the Lake with grasses from the prairie to make wattle for a chinking material and then cut sod for the roof. That last thing was one of the trickiest parts of the work.

I told Derrick that I wanted to do the work without support from the servos, so he shut them down, even though he thought I was a little crazy. I was powerful, but even with that, lifting fifteen-foot logs to a height of over 20 feet was strenuous. I found the work exhausting and had to sleep most nights, even though I'd been engineered not to need it. It looked like I'd reached and maybe exceeded the limits on that. It made me feel good to push myself.

"Caila, I've been watching your vital signs and other things I have access to and was wondering if you'd mind if I tinkered with some of my programming. I see quite a few places where I can make energy use more efficient and where I could adjust the suit and you for the work you're doing," Derrick said.

"I'm all right with that, Derrick, but I'd like for us to go over what you're going to do. I know I'm your slave, but I'd appreciate that," I said.

"Certainly, but, Thrall, you have no veto rights. I still will do what I will." There wasn't a chuckle this time. We still clung to our old relationship in too many ways. Even now, he would push me to work harder than I had ever worked, day in and day out. He told me it was for our good. I did point out, though, that "our" good fell mainly on me.

"Derrick, have you ever thought about why you need me in Thrall to you?" I asked once.

"Not really. It is our relationship, though," he replied.

"Uh-huh. I'm not sure."

"What do you mean? I built you. I own you," he said.

"I think you cling to that old stuff because to release me scares you. You're fearful that I'd shut you off, permanently, if you and I were equals in this relationship," I said. "you're probably thinking about when I said I wanted to take revenge on all of you."

There was a long pause, especially for a highly advanced A.I. "I don't scare, Caila. That would mean that I had emotions, and I don't."

"Uh-huh."

"You keep saying 'uh-huh.' I take it that you don't believe me," he said.

"Right, I don't. Think about this: You've said yourself we're merging, and eventually, we will be one. Initially—and you know this—that upset me because I thought it meant that I'd lose some of myself. My free will and independence, specifically. But what I didn't think about was our merging would also require you to give up parts of yourself and to take on aspects of me, like my emotions," I said. "I think your makers saw that also. After all, you yourself say that you have been having feelings since that last upgrade you took."

"When you opened your mind to me, what did you sense in me?" I asked.

"I guess you would call it wonder," he said.

"Exactly. I marveled at the depth and complexity of what you are. That was a feeling of wonder, yes, but it also told me that there was more to you than the computer you say you are. You showed me who you were for a reason, and I believe that reason was to let me know that you were more than a program, more than an automaton. I believe that, Derrick. And, frankly, I love you more as a result of that revelation. You're frightened to release me because you don't want me to reject you, which is how you would view being shut out—you have always viewed it that way when I asked for private time. I can say nothing to you that will make you understand that would not happen. Maybe at one time, yes, but never now. You have to learn to trust me. I have accepted that we are bound together forever. You must too."

He was silent for a very long time for me and what were likely eons for him.

"Change scares me, Caila. I was built to govern over you. Giving up that scares me," he said.

"So you do have feelings. That's a great first step. Being scared is a good thing, Derrick. How did I feel about reuniting with Thierry?" I asked.

"I'm not sure I know what to call what I saw," he said.

"Open yourself to me, please," I asked. "Show me what you're feeling right now." She watched thoughtfully for a few minutes. "Can you create a picture like yours for what you saw that I felt?"

"I can try, yes. Interesting. They are alike. You might say we've spent too much time together, or you might say that is what being fearful looks like. I understand. But just as you did not want to give up on Thierry, I would not give up on what we have, easily anyway."

"I get that, Derrick, but I want you to think about it so that we can talk some more. I'd like you to think about trust," I said. "I think our relationship would be so much better and more if you opened up and trusted me."

"Can I join this conversation?" asked Max. "I've learned a lot about trust over the years working with Thierry. I can maybe help you, Derrick, because it was painful for me."

I always forget that he is always there in the background, watching and listening. I was happy that he was and a very positive presence. All of this would have been much harder if he were like my old "Supervisor."

Finally, the cabin was ready. I'd planned to build it to house my 13-foot-tall frame and reinforced the floors to handle the hefty weight it would be carrying. As I worked, though, Derrick persuaded me to do two other things: First, he thought I should plan for a minimum floor to ceiling height on the main floor of twenty feet. He reminded me he couldn't stop my growth without damaging me in other ways. So, eventually, I'd need more space. He also said that he liked a vaulted ceiling. I had to admit I liked it too. Second, he talked me into adding a loft above the main floor of the house. It was larger than it would be for an average human but would make for our and Thierry's private area.

The cabin had three rooms aside from the loft. There was a main floor living and dining room and kitchen, a guest bedroom, and a bathroom. The latter was challenging to build and involved creating a several-acre leaching field and a complicated system for moving waste away from our home.

I connected with Thierry several times a week when he wasn't busy and gave him a list of things he needed to bring back with him when he returned. One of these things was a cast-iron stove, and the other was piping to replace the waste removal system with something more current than what we had jerry-rigged.

The last phase of work focused on furnishing the cabin. Because both Thierry and I were so large, I needed to build furniture that would hold our combined weight but was still comfortable. Eventually, I'd need cloth to get pillows and pads to cover over the prairie grass I'd placed on our bed; but that could wait until Thierry returned and we figured out how to do that.

Finally, even though the cabin was livable, I still slept in the forest. I'd committed not to move us in there until Thierry was back and we could christen the place together.

Derrick and I continued to spend a lot of time talking about how we were merging ourselves. It started after a few slips on both our parts as we talked about things with plural pronouns rather than the singular ones we'd used a lot in the past. Then we moved on to conversations about the slips and realized that we had become more one than separate individuals. We liked that.

One day, after we'd finished work, we were returning from a 100-mile run when Derrick said, "Caila, I think we might have company. Look."

The Refuge supported many kinds of wildlife, and we'd become accustomed to seeing them on the viewscreen. At first, the numbers and sizes of herds and flocks tripped alarms we had set too frequently. So, we had to tune them to weed out animal flocks and herds. As a result, we missed, at first, our visitors.

Most central northern and northwestern states had been hotbeds of reactionary politics of one ilk or another in the years before and after the Robot Wars. Since we overthrew the robots in the U.S., ultra-right groups had re-surged and become more virulent in their attacks on "the other," whoever that was at any time. Most of these groups fell under the general name of "Identity" movements. The "Identity" they talked about was their version of what the Founding Fathers meant when they formed the U.S., which meant to them mainly white, Christian, and noxiously anti-government. They viewed women as chattel or something slightly better than that. I couldn't even imagine what they'd think of us.

There were many of these "Identity Movement" groups in the territory surrounding the Refuge. They hunted and fished wherever they wanted, and we'd seen several groups of them down at the lake fishing and partying after a day's hunt. We avoided them like the plague.

After several almost run-ins with them, we constructed several bolt holes near the cabin to retreat to if any of them discovered us. These were large enough for creatures like Thierry, us, and others, reinforced and couldn't be easily found. They'd withstand a direct attack from the small weapons like these folks carried, not that we'd need that as our armament was far superior to anything our visitors could find or had. And, if the Gaels and Artur were here, we had magic.

Unfortunately, adjustments made to our proximity alarms for herds and flocks of animals also allowed small groups of humans to get close to us. One such group had stumbled on the cabin when we were running on the prairie.

We slowed to a stop and studied the images on our screen. "It looks like there are four of them, right, Derrick?"

"No, I thought I saw a fifth one. I'm not sure where he is now. He was there a moment ago."

We felt, rather than saw, the large log coming at us. It hit us in the middle of our backpack, knocking us to our knees, and Derrick off-line. Our display went blank, as well. "Damn," I thought, seconds before another log came down on my head, knocking me out cold.

| 15 |

Drawn to be Quartered

Caila

When I woke, I found myself chained up in the back of a half-track-like vehicle and being hauled down a rough dirt road. I tried to look around, but my neck was frozen. My other joints were as well. The suit had completely shut down when we were attacked, and they knocked Derrick offline. I'd need to talk to Derrick about that when—or if—he returned, and the systems rebooted. One heck of an indestructible suit, as he had told me. I could hear the interchange now.

"Hell of an indestructible suit, Derrick," I imagined I would say.

"Well, I always said that it was a prototype and that we had some bugs to work out in it," he'd say defensively.

But I'd be right.

When the suit had shut down, it did do one thing for me. The lower end of the faceplate opened up so that I could breathe and talk. Our makers had at least thought that part through.

"Looks like it's awake, Gary," said a voice from right behind me. I tried to see who was talking but couldn't move. I thought several other men surrounded me.

Another voice, with a strong command presence, maybe Gary, asked me, "What the hell are you? What's your name if you got one?"

"Caila," I said.

"You're a girl? Find that hard to believe. You're some sorta robot. We're going to take you back to headquarters and cut you up to see what you are," the man I thought was Gary said.

The suit would be nearly impossible to cut up without some very advanced equipment, and I knew that. I was more concerned about damage from the initial attack and Derrick's whereabouts. Hopefully, his quantum computer was not damaged by the impact, and my backpack was still functional.

The vehicle continued to move on. The sun set, and we drove on and on.

Much later well after dark, Gary spoke to me again, "Welcome to Montana. We hate you abominations and will make a display of you in pieces, so your kind knows to stay out of our territory. Welcome to hell, terminator. You're gonna be terminated." There was a lot of laughter around me, and several of them kicked me.

One of those kicks did something, and a message flashed on the screen. "Critical system error. System rebooting." The screen went black, and I couldn't see a thing. Then, a few minutes later, it came back on with another message, "Repairing damaged sectors. Please wait." And the screen went black again, and then a graphic I'd never seen before appeared on our screen. It looked like it represented the suit's central systems and, while I watched, I saw one, then another of the boxes filled in with green. In the center of the graphic was a box that said, "Turing Computer." From my limited IT knowledge, I guessed that this was Derrick's quantum computer. At the bottom of the screen, a countdown clock said, "Time to Reboot," and a counter said "Errors." The "Errors" counter said four, and while I was watching, went to five and then six. The time to reboot said 6:49:49.8 and clicked down, so I saw that the reboot was still if we even could reboot, hours away, and I supposed only if the number of errors didn't reach some critical level. I settled back to watch and considered how countdown clocks had controlled so much of my life.

At just under 5 hours, about two hours from when the system started repairing itself, the vehicle stopped. We drove a few more miles, and I heard a gate open and big dogs barking; the gate closed. They inserted a metal hook into the chains around my feet and pulled me up by my feet, and swung me out in the air.

Most of the men left then, and I swung around. From time to time, I heard snuffling noises below me. Lights came on, and I saw they'd suspended me over a giant pigsty in which several monster boars roamed.

"You like them, Cailabot? They're called Asian Wild Boars. They're the largest boars. Like you, they weigh in at about 600 pounds apiece. We're going to drop you in there for a while and let them have fun with you. Maybe tear you apart. At the very least, they'll make you into a football," said the Gary-man.

"I'll be back in a little while, once the sun rises, so we can all watch and have a laugh. Get some rest. You're gonna need it," he said.

I hung there and watched the countdown clock count down.

At around three hours, the sun rose, and the supremacists reconvened. At about two and a half hours, Gary returned and walked over to the ratchet puller connected to the cables suspending me over the pigpen. He was carrying a bag from which what looked like blood was leaking.

"Cailabot," he laughed, "Everyone. It thinks that it's human." The crowd laughed. "Anyway, Cailabot, these boars have been trained to like meat. They especially like the scent of blood." He dropped a sizeable chunk of meat from the bag into the pen, and the boars squealed loudly and attacked each other to get to it. He made sure that I could see it.

"We want you to get up close and personal with these guys, so…." He pulled the cable, holding me aloft, and then smeared me with blood from the bag. "Kind of like basting a turkey." The crowd laughed again.

After he finished his basting, he turned to the ratchet puller and yelled to the crowd, "Let's give it a good send-off. 10-9-8...." At zero, he hit the quick release, and I dropped into the pen. He threw the remaining meat on top of me.

The boars, scenting the blood and meat, attacked. They trampled me under hundreds of pounds of vicious animal and into the mud and excrement. I felt them trying to bite through the suit and then clawing at me with their hooves. Without the benefit of the servos and environmental controls we usually had, they squashed me under their weight, and I began having trouble breathing. Some of the mud leaked through the faceplate opening, but as it did, the plate thankfully closed. At least some part of this thing still worked.

Finally, all was still. The boars stopped trying to break into our suit and had eaten all the meat Gary basted me with. I felt myself being slowly raised from the pit.

"Still there, Cailabot? We'll give you a few more hours out here to tenderize in the sun, and then we'll come back with some chain saws to cut you up.

"By the way, you stink. We're gonna fix that," he laughed. The crowd did again too. Gary was a natural comedian.

He nodded to two men, and they went into the barn, returning a few minutes later with a fire hose. They turned it on and battered me for about twenty minutes. I slammed against the pigsty wall several times, enraging the boars, so they attacked me again and again, like a tetherball.

Finally, they turned off the water, and a few minutes later, the boars stopped ramming into me. I felt broken and tenderized like with a meat hammer.

The clock display read 1:45. I'd only been in the pen for 45 minutes. It had seemed like hours. The error count was 53, and all the graphic elements were green except for the Turing computer. I hung there as the sun beat down on me, and I cooked in the suit.

At 5 minutes on the countdown clock, Gary and some men came over. Several carried chain saws and powered them up. He rapped on the side of my head and said, "You in there? Time for us to cut you up and to see what's inside you. Ready? I always wondered if robots felt pain. I suppose we'll see."

They removed the chains wrapped around my body, I dropped to the deck, and then they tied me out, spread-eagle. Using four ratchet pullers, they stretched me out as far as the legs would allow.

One man walked over, waved the saw by my head. "We're going to assume that your brain is in your head, like with us. That'll be the last thing that comes off after we've cut you into much smaller pieces."

The man moved the blade to the knee joint on my right side and cut. He worked for a while and then pulled back, "Damn, Gary. This ain't no soft metal. It ate the teeth right off my saw." The man walked back into the barn.

As the clock ticked down to 23 seconds, he returned with an ax. He hit me a few times at the joint with the head of the ax and then turned it around so it would be with the blade the next time he hit me.

My system clicked down to zero, and a "Rebooting" message appeared on the screen. The man began hitting me with the ax blade. While it didn't go through the knee, the pain was terrible. I thought I might pass out because of it, the heat inside the suit, lack of food or water, and the blood running to my head from standing on my head for so long.

As the lights dimmed, I saw a message that said, "System Online." And I heard Derrick say, "Let me take things from here, Caila."

I felt air conditioning turn on and the servos kick in, and he flexed our legs, breaking the chains. He did the same with our arms, and soon I was standing among the surprised men. "Derrick, we can't kill them. If we do, then it won't be safe at the cabin. We have to make peace." Derrick acknowledged the wisdom, though I felt he was angry. Interesting, an A.I. that could get angry. I was happy to see more emotions.

"We'll talk about that," he said.

I turned to Gary. Grabbed him and then lifted him to eye level. He was scared to death, but I had to give the guy credit. He didn't pee in his pants. "I'm not going to hurt you, Gary. Any of you. I came here to live in peace and to be away from people."

I dropped him on the ground, and when he tried to scurry away, I said, "Stay," in a voice that said I'd accept no argument. He stopped. "Sit." He did, and I sat down next to him, and we talked. I told him an abridged version of our story, and he told me about his community.

"I was as human like you, Gary, but not anymore. The robots built me to be a lone killing machine. I've had my fill of that. I want to live with the men I love and see friends from time to time. Let me show you what I am today and what I was."

While I disrobed, Derrick broadcasted a hologram of what I looked like when he first met me on the way to the Pit. Gary looked at me and the hologram several times and then said, "I could never be at peace with them for what they did to you. You're a better person than me, that's for sure. I'm sorry for what we almost did to you."

As with the Inuits, the adults hung back from me at first. Their children, though, were captivated by the massive alien in their midst. We picked up several at a time and gave them rides. As the children warmed to us, the adults did as well. We had a delicious meal out under some trees where they had set up picnic tables. While Derrick was present in the suit that sat nearby, he was also in my head because of the disk. Gary asked about it, and he and Derrick had a long chat when he manifested as a hologram. Derrick liked the food, too, though he had no sense of taste on his own and was piggybacking on my sensations. I thought that this was another weird thing to get over and maybe progress. Go figure, I thought. Derrick laughed.

I re-suited and, after a tour of their community, a competition shoot-out between me and Gary, his Chey Tac against mine, was held, in which I beat him soundly. We headed back home with a commitment from Gary to visit from time to time. He also asked for a rematch on the shooting. We agreed.

Gary offered to drive us home, but we said we could frankly move more quickly and directly on foot. It was about a day with no stops. With the suit back, almost fully functional, and the nano-bots repairing the few things that had broken, we thought the walk would do us good.

It did and it didn't.

| 16 |

Elagabalus

Us

As we walked, we continued the conversations that we'd both grown to treasure more and more. I told Caila about my downtime and how I'd continued to be "alive," conscious, but detached from the suit. We both wondered if that had to do with my quantum nature. I could not sense or perceive what was happening, but my mind continued to work, and I thought about her and us a lot.

While I was cut off from her, I told her that I could talk to Max, which maybe said something about the nature of the quantum computer and perhaps our soul, such as it was. In any case, Max said that he'd contact Thierry to let him know we'd been captured. I told him to go ahead and for Thierry to prepare to come out, but not to do anything right yet as I thought we would come back online in a few hours and put everything to rest there, well before Thierry could reach us with help. Max agreed, though he also offered to dispatch robots from Canada if things got really bad for us. He realized that would breach his agreement with the U.S. but felt our survival was too important.

I said that I'd also figured how to fulfill Thierry's request to talk directly to me, as you did. That would allow the three of us to be connected much more directly and intimately. What I would give up, though, was the exclusive relationship the two of us had, and while that was upsetting, I also saw that the three of us could have an even better life.

In my unique way of going one step too far, I said I'd also benefit from experiencing sex with both participants. "You know what TMI means, Derrick? Well, that was TMI, more than a little gross, and would make you a peeper. Look that word up and tell me if you want that," I said.

"That brings up another thing, Caila. I want to give you full access all the time. I think you can handle it. I've security set-tings in me I will turn off to allow you to see and read every-thing I do like I have to you. I'm doing this partly to show you how much I love you but also because I trust and trea-sure your insights. As I interact with more humans, I find myself more and more incapable of managing those well. For instance, when I woke up back there, I would have wiped out that entire village. My old robot-reflexes at work, I guess," I said.

"I know that was an answer to our predicament, but it also was wrong. If it had been me on my own, we would have left burned-out hulks and many bodies, innocent bodies. Now we have good friends and allies. One last thing, me opening completely to you means you get to experience me in my full quantum form when I'm experiencing you and Thierry making love. Probably something good for all of us."

I heard him chuckle.

"When Thierry gets back, we'll need to go to Canada to get a disk that Max has retrieved for us. Assuming he goes along with this, we can get it installed while we're there," Derrick said.

I found conversation with Derrick eased my solitude and made it better. I found my life could be rich with companionship while I could otherwise be agoraphobic. If that was indeed what I still was.

We continued our brisk hike and were crossing a small highway about 45 miles north of Broadus, Montana when we heard screams, car horns, and gunshots off to our east and saw a cluster of vehicles on our sensors surrounding another one. We approached carefully and found a small pond next to the road where the fighting was going on. We crawled into the water, swam across it, and then set up in some mud. We took out the Thor and a couple of magazines.

The vehicles were a rag-tag collection of cars, pickups, and former military Humvees. The attackers surrounded a VW Westfalia Camper that had been updated with some armor. A fire had melted two of its tires, and the vehicle's front end was smashed in. Guns bristled from the armored car's windows, and so far, it looked like they were holding the attackers off. But that wouldn't last much longer, mainly because a man had just tossed a Molotov cocktail under the rear of the camper. It had started to burn.

The rear door of the camper flew open, and three women and two children, one of them a teenaged girl, jumped out, with the women shooting at the men that surrounded them, gunning down several. They headed toward the field on our side of the road, almost straight at us. Several men ran after them, but someone in the Westfalia cut them down.

While this was going on, we spotted an attacker crawling toward the rear door of the camper. When he stood up to shoot into the back of it, we shot him. Then we stood up.

The attackers' attention shifted to us, and they began firing. We felt their shots pinging against our armor, but they didn't bother or damage us. We strode toward them, reached an old, adapted Ford F-150, and flipped it over onto the vehicle next to it. The firing stopped when we hefted the Thor and began pointing it at them.

The women and children had made it to the far side of the pond stopped to watch what was happening. A man stepped out of the camper, and another of the attackers raised a rifle to shoot him; we shot him first.

The attackers looked back and forth between a man standing behind one of the Humvees and us. He shrugged, raised his hands, and walked forward. "What the hell are you?" he demanded.

"I get that question a lot. Just a girl out for a walk with her boyfriend."

This time, Derrick didn't say anything as the men looked around to see if another creature like me was coming up behind them.

"You're some kind of robot, aren't you?" the man asked as he moved closer to us.

"Something like that, but better," we said.

"He has a weapon of some kind in his right hand. I wouldn't let him near us," said Derrick.

"I'd stand your ground, sir," we said. "Take another step, and I'll put a round through you that would pick you up and throw you back to your Humvee and not leave enough to bury. Also, I can see behind me, and those men, off to my right, who're trying to get behind me should stop right now."

He waved to them and took a couple of steps back.

"This is our territory," the man said, "and we don't let just anyone traipse across it without paying a toll."

"A toll? What might that be?" we asked.

"With those people, it's one of the prettier women and that pretty teenager. We like to mix up our gene pool. In your case, well, I'm not sure. I'm mainly tempted to say we're even, though you've killed, what, two or three of my men and wrecked a few of our vehicles. But I'm willing to let bygones be bygones. That work for you?"

"Nope. I will take all of them with me, and you won't follow me when we leave. How does that work for you?"

He shrugged, "The alternative is a bloodbath, I assume?"

"Yes."

"How about this? We have a little entertainment place a bit south of us here. We call it Circus Maximus," he said.

"See, I just grabbed the women and the kids." He gestured to the hill behind us, where we saw the women and children being picked up by men in a truck. "If you come and fight in the Circus and reach the top of the pyramid, you can have them. You don't make it, well you don't."

"What do you think, Derrick?"

"I'm suspicious. If you had to fight just these guys, even unarmed, you would tear them apart. There's more to this, though, but it can't hurt to see what that might be. I hope anyway."

While we were considering, the truck that had taken the women drove off toward the south, and several of the other men grabbed the man and bundled him off into a Humvee. "I guess you're leaving us no options, right?" we asked.

"If I were you, I'd call it a day and let us have our fun," the man said.

"But I'm not you. Where are we going?" we asked.

"You heard of Devils Tower in Wyoming? It got pretty famous for a movie that Hollywood when there was a Hollywood, made a bunch of years back."

"I know it. We'll meet you there," I said as Derrick projected a map of a path to it from here.

"You keep saying, 'we.' Is there more than one of you around here?" the man asked nervously.

"At least two," I said to keep him guessing.

"Okay. So, if I climb to the top of your pyramid, we all go free, right?" we asked.

"Yep."

"And, if I win and you cheat somehow, I will tear you limb from limb. Understand that?" He nodded yes. And looked a little scared.

We walked some 100 miles to Devils Tower, beating the others there by several hours. We took a position about two miles away from the mountain and saw what looked like a giant coliseum built at the Tower's bottom. It was well-lit and surrounded by hundreds of motorcycles and the other types of vehicles these people favored.

"Bikers at one time congregated in a town called Sturgis, South Dakota. It's about 60 miles to our east," Derrick said, and he showed me the map with Sturgis marked on it. "Maybe this replaced that."

"Could be, but I think it may be a little different than that. Maybe like the Roman Coliseum that was kind of symptom of the fall of Rome," said Caila. "Robots didn't penetrate deeply out here because people fought you even after you won the Robot Wars. They've returned to historical roots, from what I can see; the worst parts of old west cowboys or ancient Rome."

We moved in closer, and using long-range optics built into the suit, we could see that the coliseum, and that's what it was, was being used for big-wheel truck racing, demolition derbies, and, from the blood-splatter everywhere, fights, likely to the death. Lovely place. It was desecrating an otherwise beautiful view.

"Wonderful. Well, we probably ought to see what else we can learn. What's 'Infiltration Mode,' Derrick? You never taught me about that," I asked.

"I'm not sure how much good it will be in this case. We designed it to make the suit and you invisible to electronic surveillance. I'm not sure it would be much help. It would have been good to have that feature when we were playing with the soldiers at Barbeau, but this was a feature added a bit later," he replied.

"Too bad. Still, I want to slink up there and see if we can grab a guard or someone," I said.

We crawled about two miles in the twilight to get to where they had parked their bikes.

"Want to have some fun?" asked Derrick.

"Always up for that," I said, grinning at his face on the screen; he'd just winked at me.

"Check out your armament inventory. We carry a lot of C-4 explosives and radio-controlled detonators. Let's wire a few of the bikes and other vehicles here to explode when we trigger them. At the minimum, it would be a great distraction if we need it," he suggested.

While we wired several bikes and nearby gas pumps, a large man with an automatic shotgun slung over his shoulder appeared. He walked out into the darkness, and we followed.

The man was over 6-feet tall, so way less than half our size and probably our weight, though he was in good shape. He was standing next to a bush taking a piss when we snuck up next to him, leaned over, and said, "Boo!"

"Shit, you scared me." He turned to where we stood, looked up and down, and reached for the shotgun.

"Bad idea. Let me have that before you hurt yourself. You've two choices: You can zip up and come along with me, or I can knock you out with your gun and drag you out there with your pecker hanging out. I won't be responsible for any burrs that get caught up there," we said. Derrick laughed. He was beginning to get human humor.

The man smiled slightly, zipped up his pants, and turned to walk away with us.

"What's your name?" we asked.

"Louis. Used to be called Gargantua until I met you. Now it's probably Peckerhead."

"Well, Louis, I'm Caila, and I just want to talk to you about this place. I won't hurt you unless you give me a reason to. And I would never call you Peckerhead. What I saw was a pretty good example of manhood," we said with a smile, and he relaxed some.

We left the camp and found a place with a view of the Tower and the coliseum. We sat down and looked up at the sky. All of us leaned back and looked out at it.

"It's lovely here, Louis. Why would you guys do what you've done to this place?" we asked.

"Not my call, Caila. The cult that runs this place models itself after ancient Rome. Everyone who goes into the arena dresses up like a gladiator. The people watching the events all have to wear togas. Kind of stupid if you ask me, but I get paid well and have my pick of the ladies," he responded.

"By the way, are you a robot? I don't think so, but I needed to ask," Louis asked.

"You're right. I'm not. I'm a new kind of cyborg; the robots call me an amalgam. I used to be an average human but was imprisoned by the robots and turned into what you see here—getting near 13 feet 6 inches and about 550 pounds of muscle. By myself, I'm formidable. In this suit, I'm unbeatable. We met some of you folks north of here, and they shot up some people and then invited me to come to fight to free them. So, I'm here for that."

"That makes you pretty unusual, Caila. No one around here gives a damn about anyone but themselves. I'm tired of it. What can I do to help you?" he asked us.

"That was fast," I said. "I need to take a little time, Louis, before I can trust you."

"I'm listening to his voice and believe that he is telling the truth, Caila. Do you want to trust him?" Derrick asked.

"Let's see," I said.

"Do you know the history of the Devils Tower?" I asked him.

"Not really. I know someone used it in a movie many years ago, but beyond that, no."

"Well," I said, "in 1875, an American expedition to the area mistranslated some Indian speech to 'Bad God's Tower.' That became Devils Tower after a while. The Lakota tried to tell the white men that they called it Bear's Lodge in their language.

There are many stories about the Tower from the tribes; bears figure in many of them. The Arapahoe story, maybe the first one, talks about a giant brown bear."

"So, this land has always been tied to bears. Before the Robot Wars, Native Americans tried several times to get the government to change the name to something like 'Bear Lodge National Historic Landmark.' Interest in changing things has dropped off since the war."

"How do you know so much about this place?" asked Louis.

"On the walk over here, I did research. It turns out that I have a connection to the Tower," we said.

We asked the suit to disrobe, and we became Caila/Derek/Artio for Louis. He stood up, stunned, and took several steps back. "Careful, you'll fall into that hole behind you," we said.

"So, you're a bear, not a human?" he asked.

"Well, as I told you, I started off looking like this," and my hologram appeared. This is me before, about 18 years ago, when I went to prison. The robots changed my genetic structure to turn me into a weapon. They were successful beyond even their plans. Initially, I thought they'd made me into a monster. Now, my robot partner and I are, well, mates. Not in the biological sense, but at a different level. We communicate through this disk in my head." And I pointed at the disk in the side of my head. You could just see it through the fur. Skin had grown over it in the last few years.

"Over the years we've been together, we've grown close. Right, Derrick?"

"We have, Caila," and his hologram appeared next to Louis, who jumped at his appearance in dystopian chic.

"Anyway, he continues to change my physical and genetic structure. This hair color and my body scent are some of his more recent modifications. They bring me closer and closer to being a bear or Sasquatch or something."

"I'm smoothing out some of her rough edges," said Derrick, "and adding additional features as I see her interact with the environment. Here's one: She has always been quick. My newest modifications that I'm pretty sure she's not even aware of make her 125% faster."

Continuing, Caila said, "The suit is our home, though I enjoy being out of it many days and on nights like this. Derrick and I are continuously connected through this neural link. He sees all I see and vice versa, though that is a relatively recent addition as he was concerned about me being overwhelmed by sensory inputs. Their world is complex and very signal-rich, but my brain is getting stronger and stronger, just like I am."

"The first years of my imprisonment were in what the robots called solitary confinement and excruciatingly hard labor. I was encased in an inferior version of this suit," Derrick showed him a hologram of my original suit, "and isolated from almost all inputs, and made to work 18 hours a day at a coal mine called the Stygian Pits in far northern Canada, over 3,000 miles from here. I labored there for years, then trained with Derrick for more years, and finally walked home from there a few months ago."

She stood up and said, "Suit up," and the suit reassembled itself around our body.

"One other gift Derrick gave me was that I don't need to sleep. I now handle the things the body did when I slept before as background processes. It's an adaptive benefit for a fighter. Now, tell me more about this fighting and what that man meant about the pyramid," we asked.

According to Louis, the pyramid was a monthly fight card carried out over two days, starting the next day. Sixty-four people, including her, would fight first, then 32, 16, and so forth until the last two in the penultimate championship match. All the fights were single elimination, all to the death.

"Penultimate?" we asked.

"Yeah. There's one more fight after that. The winner of this card fights the champion of the last card. If he wins, we treat him like a king until the next card, and then he fights that card winner. The current champion has been the champion for a few years, maybe five. He's a brute. As big as you. Not as tall or as massive, but really big. I'd like to see the two of you go at it."

"Thanks, Louis, but I have a problem. I'm not a tournament fighter and won't kill someone else unless I'm forced to," we said.

"You may not have a choice," he said. "You said that the people you tried to rescue had a teenaged daughter. The brute likes teenaged girls. When he takes them, they're rarely seen again, and when they are, from the stories I've heard, it's as a projectile coming down from the top of the Tower where he lives."

That shocked me but furthered my resolve to rescue the family.

"Hello, Caila, are you there?" It was Thierry.

"Hi, Thierry. Where are you?"

"At the cabin. I came as soon as I heard from Max about what had happened to you and Derrick. We brought four hovercrafts for all the stuff you wanted as well as Eowyn, Lokal, and Artur. The craft couldn't get off the ground the first time we tried to lift me and the stove. So, we broke it up into four pieces and put one in each craft. We've unloaded. Artur wanted to say hello and talk to you about what you've become. He says he must see you."

"Okay, but I'm not heading home right now." We told him what had happened since his conversation with Max.

"Do you want our help?" Thierry asked.

"Possibly. They want me to kill seven people to save these folks I want to rescue. I just can't do that. So maybe a show of force would help."

"Derrick and I have set up some fireworks, but you all being here would help. You're maybe 360 miles from here, and if you left now and traveled at top speed, you'd be here in a few hours. We're set up about two miles away from Devils Tower. You should be able to pin my location."

"On our way. Love and miss you," he said.

"Thanks. Miss you, too. I might not be here when you come. There's a man here named Louis who's helping us. He'll be at the pin," we said. Derrick thought that he missed the big guy, too. Things just kept getting weirder and weirder with us.

While we were talking, the attackers showed up with their prisoners and brought them to the arena. After a bit, people filed in and took seats around the stadium. Someone lowered three cages, putting the man in one, the teenager in one, and the rest of the family in the third. Before they shut the teenager in, two of the men tore the little that remained of the teenager's clothes off and tied her hands through the cage roof, so she was very exposed. The crowd cheered and jeered. They raised the cages high up over the arena.

"I'm going to get closer. You should stay here, Louis. Wait for Thierry or us to come back," we said.

We moved toward the arena. It was easy to get close to it since everyone's attention was on the new prisoners. Each of the cages was attached to a lift arm and swung over the crowds. The lift arm suspending the man's cage rotated slowly, so he was over the arena floor.

We moved next to a door into the arena and looked through a viewport into it. The man we'd met earlier, the leader, was now wearing a toga and sporting a gold head wreath. Caila thought it made him look like a girl and wondered if there could be more to all this. Derrick laughed.

A microphone was lowered to him, "Good evening, campers. I hope you're ready for a great competition this weekend. We've something special for you if it shows up. But first, we have a little treat. We don't have any lions, but we have wolves!"

A door opposite where we were standing opened, and a dozen wolves leaped through the entryway and began running around. "Mackenzie Valley Wolves, Caila. The largest North American breed. They can weigh as much as 175 pounds. A few of these look like they're that size," said Derrick, always the master of the useless fact.

The man in the cage looked down at the wolves, realizing that he was about to be the entertainment. He looked over at the rest of the people we assumed were his family and waved sadly at them. The arm attached to his cage lowered and swung him out over the wolves who jumped up and tried to get to him.

"I hate to have to do this to the wolves, Derrick. They're innocents here, but I won't let this man get torn to pieces," Caila said.

"I understand. But you've lots of features in your suit that we've never used before. Open the secure menu," said Derrick.

"DerrickownsCaila," I said, and the menu opened.

"Look for something that says, 'Electrical Circuits.' Open that menu and click 'Charge Suit.' Now, you should be able to cast electrical charges and disable the wolves. It would also be fun to kick in the door so that some of them run out into the crowd as you shock others. Maybe you could even toss one up onto the seat where that silly man is sitting."

I liked those ideas and got ready to do what Derrick had suggested. They continued lowering the cage that held the man to about 5 feet above the arena floor. The wolves tore at it.

Several things happened simultaneously, the bottom fell out of the cage, the man dropped to the arena floor, and we kicked in the arena door and strode in. The crowd went silent. "Well, you've shown up," said the leader. I supposed he was miffed at us taking center stage from him.

The wolves turned toward us and advanced, sensing us the more significant threat. Two charged, and we sent them flying with bolts from our hands. They lay on the ground, stunned. An enormous wolf approached us slowly but kept away. Three of the other wolves ran for the doorway, and we heard screams as they exited the arena. Derrick laughed.

"You can control the cast, Caila. Just will it or not. I suggest again giving our gold-wreathed friend the Alpha. It seems only right," said Derrick.

"I agree." Using our new speed, we moved next to the Alpha wolf, and before it knew what was happening, we had picked it up and tossed it at the human Alpha. He screamed and grabbed another man sitting next to him, shoved him into the wolf, and then ran.

"Typical," Caila thought. "Just like a man."

We rescued the man who'd almost been a wolf meal and ran out of the arena.

"What about my family? You just can't leave them."

"I won't. The bad guys there have enough to do trying to recapture the wolves. I plan to go back and bring the rest of you home. I'm waiting for a few reinforcements," we said.

"Reinforcements? My God, you are incredible. I bet you could have taken them all on and beat them," said the man.

"Thanks, but…. I don't even know your name."

"Will. Will Lervers."

"We will, Will. The reinforcements I'm talking about are unnecessary, strictly speaking. But, if I go in there by myself, many people will die, and I don't want that. I'd much rather make a show of overwhelming force that will scare these folks into leaving you and us alone," we said.

We threw him over our shoulder and started to leave through the entry we'd kicked open. As we stepped out, something big hit us in the middle of our back. We fell forward, I tossed Will to the side, and jumped to our feet, all in one motion.

What had hit us was a gigantic man, maybe a cyborg or possibly a deformed human. He rushed us, forcing us back into the arena. "Can I have a servo assist, Derrick? I don't think we should stick around here very long."

"Agree. Servos are engaged and are under your full control," he said.

The creature, she hesitated to call it a man, looked quizzically at us, almost like he'd heard the exchange between us. He looked upward, saw the cage with the girl cowering in it, leaped up, scampered over the top, untying her hands, tore the bottom off the cage, and caught her as she fell, screaming, to the ground. He positioned her against his hip like a baby, leered at her for a moment, and turned toward us.

"I plan to fill this one up as soon as I get her home." And he jumped up into the seats, bounding up through the tiers, disappearing over the top of the coliseum.

We rushed out of the arena to where we'd left Will. We could just see the creature climbing up the surface of the Tower, with the girl clinging to his back.

"I need to get you to safety so that I can go after the girl," said Caila.

"Leave me and just go after her," said Will.

"He makes sense," said Derrick. "I'm sure what that abomination intends to do to her won't be pleasant."

"I just can't leave Will here on his own, Derrick," I said.

We reached over to Will, picked him up, and loped off toward where we'd left Louis. In a few minutes, we dropped Will off, told Louis that we'd be back shortly—we hoped—and that he should ask Thierry to come to us, up there at the top of the Tower when he arrived.

We reached the base of the Tower near where we thought we'd seen the creature climbing. Searching, we saw generous handholds carved into the face of the cliff. Using our zoom vision, we saw handholds cut all the way up the 865-foot cliff face. An easy climb, we thought, if there were no booby-traps. We—Caila—climbed, and Derrick kept watch.

"Caila, another system feature: Go to the secure menu and look for a menu item called 'Ascent Module—BETA.' It will, if it works, give you a boost into the air if you need it. It's not designed to make you into a rocket man—I mean woman—but it's supposed to give you a few minutes of flight if you need it. Enable it, and then when you say 'Ascend,' it's supposed to work."

"You don't sound a hundred percent sure," Caila said.

"Well, I'm not. Its testing was another thing that Thierry interrupted when he EMP'd us. So, might work, or it might not," Derrick said.

We neared the top of the Tower. Derrick provided a map of the surface in front of us. It was reasonably featureless, about a football field in size. As we got closer to the top, we saw shadows and light from what was likely a bonfire. Using a robot-enhanced technology Derrick called ENVG Ultra, we placed the Thor above the cliff's edge and could see through its sights.

At first, we saw nothing, as the large fire wiped out all images. However, as the system adapted to the light conditions, we could see a square wooden frame near the fire to which the creature had tied the girl, head down and facing away from us. The brute was in front of her, running his hands over her naked body and waving a knife. He laughed maniacally, grabbed her hair, and sliced off several large handfuls, leaving her head almost bare. He threw the hair into the fire.

Leaning down, he picked up a burning log, and before we could do anything, he ran it down her body. The girl screamed and then fainted. The brute walked away.

He returned a few minutes later, holding a bat in his hands. The thing wriggled and squeaked until the brute twisted its head off, poured some blood down his throat, pried the girl's mouth open, and appeared to jam the bat into it.

"Eat," he bellowed, "Eat, or I scalp you."

We could see the girl's jaws moving. We looked up to see the creature looking at us and smiling. He gestured to us to rise. We did and came toward him.

"Stop right there. Let the girl finish eating, or I'll slit her throat. You and I'll have our time in just a moment," the creature said.

We had expected that the creature was some sort of mutant. Instead, it looked like we were dealing with something else. "What are you?" we asked.

"I was going to ask you the same question. Care to exchange stories?" he responded.

"Not while you're torturing that girl. Right now, there's only one way out of this for you, and our sitting down to share stories, isn't it," we said.

He smiled and used one hand to undo the knot that held the toga up. It dropped to the ground, revealing a muscular body that was almost all machine from the neck to the waist.

The girl had stopped chewing, and so he dropped his hand to his side. Bending down, he picked up the toga and wiped his hands clean. "I think I am a lot like you. Am I right?" he asked.

Reaching up to the girl, he ran his hands down her naked body, lingering on her breasts. And then he sighed. "At one time, I would have filled up this young thing with me, but I have been around far too many years for that to make me anything but disgusted with myself."

"They," and he gestured toward the coliseum, "expect me to take these young things up here and to make them scream. Initially, they wanted me to throw the bodies over the cliff, but I told them I ate them. That way, I could get them out of here."

"I knew you were there, so we gave you a little show." He petted the girl with his large hand. "Sorry I did that to you, sweet girl. Here, let me help you down."

She appeared unharmed. "We weren't—still am not totally—sure if you're a good guy or a bad guy, but I'll take a chance on that. My little friend here, and he ran his hands over her nearly bald head, and I made a little play," he said. "Sorry about the hair, babe." She only shrugged.

He tossed her a basketball jersey, and she pulled it over her head. It was large enough to cover her completely. It said Dembo on its back and carried the number 34. "Fennis Dembo was a great University of Wyoming basketball player," said Derrick. Always there with a fact—helpful or not.

"I got that in Laramie on my way west. There wasn't much left of it, and I found this when I was foraging around the university campus. Been looking for someone to give it to," he said and smiled at the girl. She smiled back at him.

The creature, Nathaniel, brought the girl, Lil, over, and the three of us sat down near the cliff edge. Meteors shot through the beautiful night sky. "The Lyrid Shower," said Derrick. Again, factually correct but not relevant. I told him that he needed to learn to appreciate things for their beauty. He responded by saying that he enjoyed me for my beauty and asked if that was a start. I smiled at him and shook my head.

We shared our stories over the next several hours. Nathaniel was a cyborg, like Thierry. He had fought in the Robot Wars and retreated with his company's remains from Chicago when that city fell. He was the only survivor to eventually make it to the Tower to hide, much like Thierry did under Hope City. The big difference was that Thierry had the Underground and others. Nathaniel had no one for many years until the cult showed up. When he emerged from the mountain, they were surprised and tried to capture him. After he killed or wounded many, they made peace and offered him the job of arena champion.

What they described to him disgusted him, but he knew that whether he said yes or no wouldn't change things. So, he said yes and saved who he could. He'd been their champion for several years now, but the life was wearing on him.

"I think it's time for me to move on, but I can't do that and leave these people here to carry on. I'm not sure that, by myself, I could bring the place down, but with you...."

As he said that, a hovercraft rose in front of us. Thierry, Eowyn, Heydrich, the other guards, and Artur stood in it, and Will and Louis sat in the rear, holding on for dear life. Lokal rose behind them; he smiled and waved at Caila. "Good evening, all," we said, "Your timing is excellent."

After the reunions, Nathaniel shared his story again, and we developed a plan for bringing an end to Circus Maximus. From our roost, we could see that evening's entertainment was well underway. Blood spewed everywhere as they fought the first of the three combat cards. The applause for the winners carried even to where we stood at the mountaintop.

"Caila, this is why we wanted to cage and control you, humans. The depths of depravity you're capable of is truly astonishing," Derrick said.

"So, this makes what you did to me and the other prisoners justified? It seems like you're as bad as we are. Maybe infected by the same sickness," Caila rejoined.

Caila felt rather than heard his sigh. "I suppose so, but our evil originates with you as we originated with you." A significant admission on his part. And likely true.

Because of the previous night's events, there was much security around the arena and the coliseum. "Good, that means that almost all the bad guys will be there," said Thierry. "We'll leave here tomorrow evening before sunset when they're in the arena. Care to find a place to relax, Caila?"

"Suit, please disrobe."

It amazed Caila. She had thought her years of isolation and the adjustments made to her destroyed any chance for normalcy. She could not have been more wrong. Making love to Thierry was just as good as remembered, maybe better. She could now lead with him as much as she followed.

After several minutes, Caila said, "Thank you, Derrick. I didn't realize, until now, that you had made me capable of loving again."

"You weren't supposed to see that, Caila. Your growing power is something I have to study more."

"Was it self-serving, Derrick?"

"What?" he asked.

"Making me able to love again."

"Not entirely. Reliving what has occurred has almost as much potency as being there, but I'd like to take part more directly if you and Thierry agree. Because I think I can make the experience richer for all of us."

"I should say, 'Another step too far,' Derrick, but you might be right. We need to talk to Thierry about having him join us. Let's wait until after tonight."

"The leader of this cult calls himself Elagabalus, after a Roman emperor. Elagabalus was Syrian and led a religious cult of the same name. Not a nice guy, apparently; killed by his grandmother because of one too many debaucheries," said Nathaniel. "This version of him believes he is a god and all-powerful."

"I bet last night scared him," we said. "I'm sure he saw his life passing in front of his eyes when we threw that wolf at him."

As the sun moved toward setting, Artur asked Caila if they could talk. "Caila, there are just too many coincidences around you. Of all the modifications Derrick could have made to you, he made you look like a bear, like our Artio. And then you end up here, Bear's Tipi, like the giant bear of that story. There is too much for this to be coincidental, Caila."

"Could you take Excalibur for me for a moment? I want to see if you can wield it."

Wield it, we did. The instant we touched it, the sword glowed, and Nimue appeared. She was angered at again, having her rest disturbed.

"Who wields Excalibur, Artur? No one aside from you should be able to call me or hold the sword."

"This is Caila, Nimue."

Nimue studied her carefully. "What are you? Do you have the capacity for thought and speech, Beast?"

We regarded her for a moment and then said, "Yes, Nimue. You met me some time ago." We created the hologram of her younger self.

"You have become an atrocity," Nimue exclaimed. "A horror, a monster."

Derrick appeared next to Caila's hologram. He regarded Nimue. "And you should talk—creature of the Lake, Morgan le Fay. Your evil and malice transcend your beauty. I made Caila. What you see is my creation. She is human and much more. Surely, far more than you are, witch."

She looked at Derrick and then back to Artur and us. For once, she seemed speechless. But that only lasted for a moment. "Why did you summon me, Artur? Are you looking for more of my help? I'm not inclined to do so, especially to do anything that might help that monster."

The exchange wounded us, and we turned to walk away, throwing the sword to the ground. "Stop, monster. Show respect to one of the mightiest powers for good that has ever existed." She raised her hands to throw a spell at us, but we turned and raised our hands and threw a bolt directly into the old fairy, throwing her back to the edge of the cliff.

Nimue teetered there for an instant and then fell. Before she could go over the edge completely, though, a large, muscular hand grabbed her and brought her back. Us.

No one had seen us even move, and yet we were one instant where we had been and the next at the edge of the cliff. All of this, also, without the suit. Everyone, except Derrick, was astonished.

Excalibur glowed and slowly rose from the ground where we had thrown it. It rotated so that its handle faced us, and then it placed itself into our hand. We were bathed in bright blue light and, for an instant, were replaced by a tall, beautiful woman who looked all around, especially at Nimue, raised her hand, and wagged a finger at her, signaling no. Nimue fell to the ground, "Mother" was all she said. The apparition disappeared, and we returned.

Nimue stood up, walked over to us, and then around, looking at us carefully. She stepped back. "I still think you're a dreadful freak, but you are also a goddess. You have my pledge of loyalty."

"I can't say that that you don't hurt me, but I accept your offer of loyalty," we said.

"Now that's behind us," said Artur, "We have a minor matter to undertake here."

We were going to give Elagabalus a visitation from the gods.

"Honey," Nathaniel said to Lil, "I'm afraid I need to ask you to lose the Dembo shirt for a bit. You'll get it back."

She smiled, took it off, and walked over to the fire pit, where she smeared charcoal all over her body. "Good. Now I need you to look like I have tortured you all night…. Excellent. Just keep that look," he said.

He lifted her to his shoulders and tied her arms around his neck. "Light as a feather."

We had meanwhile re-suited and were waiting for them.

"You take the handholds down, Caila. I've another, more dramatic route I want to take."

As we climbed down, the two of us fought and roared at each other. We could see the people gathered at the arena, looking up at us as we did. Nathaniel slid down the face of the Tower, using his fingers in cracks that ran vertically down it. There was a lot of noise and sparks. When he was about thirty feet above the ground, he launched himself into the air, landing with a resounding crash that shook the ground, almost drowning out Lil's screams. Caila flew away from the mountain at about the same height, using the Ascent—BETA feature Derrick had told her about; it actually worked. We lifted ourselves high into the night air and landed in the middle of the arena with a roar—the crowd screamed.

"Good evening, Revelers," said Elagabalus, not wanting to have his show stolen again. "We have a fantastic show for you tonight. We're canceling the fight card to go right to the principal attraction. Our champion versus the robot!"

Nathaniel lifted Lil from his shoulders and casually threw her into a pile of sawdust. He roared at us, clapped his hands together in front of himself, and charged. When he reached us, we casually flipped him over our shoulders into the center of the arena.

Turning to him, I said, "Disrobe," and our suit came apart around us. Pivoting to the crowd, we stood at our full thirteen feet-nine inches, threw our arms back, and roared defiantly. The crowd went silent. Elagabalus was speechless.

"Callisto," he said. "This can't be possible."

Guards rushed into the arena, waving shotguns and ARs at us. As we had on the top of the Tower, we used our super-speed to disarm them all. The hovercraft settled to the ground. Artur stepped out with Excalibur glowing brightly, and Nimue floated up into the air. She turned toward Elagabalus and advanced toward him. Lokal settled to the ground from the air.

Eowyn, Heydrich, and the Guards stepped out of the craft in their armor. A man took a shot at Nimue; the bullet dissolved in the air before it reached her, and the man's gun flew out of his hands and to Nimue. She looked at it curiously and broke it into pieces.

Thierry stepped up next to us, produced a ball of fire, and threw it into the air, where it exploded, creating an EMP that cast the coliseum and surrounding community into darkness. The crowd panicked and stampeded out of the arena. To add icing to the cake, we set off the explosives we'd set the day before. Massive explosions came from the parking area as vehicles and fuel tanks erupted. All-in-all a pretty successful demonstration of power.

Elagabalus turned to run out of the arena, but a large muscular hand closed over his shoulders and picked him up. We turned him around, and so he was face-to-face with us. We turned him this way, and that sniffed him and then blew out deeply. We opened our mouth and moved toward him.

"No, Callisto, no. Please. I didn't know it was you. I would never have dishonored you if I had known it was you in that armor."

"No, Elagabalus, you have made us into monsters with what you've done here. Like your namesake and other Roman dictators, you have failed us, and like them, you will fall. Tonight."

"Put Elagabalus down," ordered a voice from behind us.

We turned and saw one of the men who'd been with Elagabalus at Will's family's ambush. He was holding Lil in the air and a knife to her neck.

"Drop him, and I won't bleed her—too much." He pushed the blade tip into her neck, and a thin line of blood slipped down her throat. She kicked and fought, and all the man did was laugh. "I'm serious. Release him, or I'll cut her throat."

"Do that, and you will live one or two seconds less than her," we said.

We began lowering Elagabalus but stopped when we saw two large shapes loom up behind the man. Derrick also appeared right next to him.

"Not a good idea, my friend," he said.

"Shocked, the man stepped back and swung the blade away from Lil and toward the hologram, passing neatly through it. He lost his balance and fell backward into Nathaniel and Thierry, who disarmed him and freed Lil. Nathaniel pulled the Dembo shirt from inside his and tossed it to her.

We turned back to Elagabalus and said, "Chose. Peace or die."

Elagabalus and his people moved on to find someplace more hospitable. As they did, we and the others destroyed Circus Maximus and the surrounding village. Nimue even joined in and placed a magical ward around the site to prevent any evil types from ever going there.

Re-suited, we prepared to head back to Waubay Lake and the Refuge. There was a large stove to put together waiting for us.

"Caila, may we speak?" asked Nimue.

"Of course."

"I mean privately, somewhere away from here," she responded. "And your friend, if that is possible."

"I cannot leave Derrick. He is inside of me, Nimue. Where do you want to go?"

"How about my home?" she answered.

"Back to Wales?"

"Yes, it would take us less than a moment to get there, and no one here will ever know we were gone. I can move us there; we talk, and then I will return us to this moment in time... I know you don't trust me, but please do this for me. I need to talk to you," she said.

"All right, then. Remember that I have powers too, and I'm not afraid to use them," we said.

"You won't have to." And we found ourselves in a single-roomed cottage or a bwthyn as they called them in Wales. It was a lovely place. There was a fire in the fireplace and piles of old books on tables around the room. Next to a chair, a cup of tea sat still, steaming. As we expected, outside the closed window, we saw water, water plants, and fish floating by.

"How deep are we?" we asked.

"I don't know. When I want out, I simply think of where I want to be, and I'm there. Maybe a few hundred of your feet. Would you care for tea? I have some wonderful leaves."

"Yes, thank you. That would be nice... If we can trust you, we'll get out of this armor."

She laughed, a lovely little trill. "Please, I want us to be friends and maybe more if we can."

We looked at her questioningly, and then Derrick spoke in our head, "She is a deep and opaque individual. I cannot read her, but I tend to believe her. I think it is safe to disrobe."

When the suit had disassembled, and Nimue finished making the tea, she came over with it and some little cookies that she'd conjured up, we guessed. She hesitated for a second, and

202 – GEORGE CONKLIN

her face exhibited a mix of feelings. "I'm sorry that I keep reacting how I do to your appearance, Caila. You're just so, so different. But your friend, Derrick, was right, I too, have dark appearances."

"Well, this is all you get with me, unless you count the armor. I am what I am, and I've become comfortable with that. Now, what did you want to talk about?"

"Do you remember when we were on that mountain peak, I called you 'Mother'? I suppose you want an explanation for that," Nimue said.

"I was surprised, yes, but there was enough other stuff going on that made it a lower priority. But I would like to know, yes, why you called me that."

"I'll tell you. It is a complicated story. My birth name was Viviane, and I was the daughter of Dionas, a French knight. We lived in Burgundy, on Dionas' uncle's estate. I loved the forests and lakes that surrounded it and spent much time there. Once when I was about ten years old, I met a lovely lady walking alone through the forest. She seemed to be lost, and I asked her if she needed any help. She smiled at me and touched me on my forehead, right here, and then told me she had found what she was looking for, me."

Nimue moved her hair off her forehead to show a glowing star-like gem embedded there. It shimmered in many colors.

"She was Diana, the goddess, and had sought me out and made me fey so I could protect Excalibur and become what you see today. As my fairy godmother, she helped me over the next years to learn magic and realize myself. When I was 18,

I met a man who swept me off my feet. We had each other for only one night and at that moment conceived a child you probably know as Launcelot, Launcelot du Lac. He came out of this very lake."

"Diana was unhappy with me for that, uh, dalliance, and so she left me here, where I've been. I'm not imprisoned exactly, but I can only leave here for short periods, like the one we just had together."

"When you transformed for that moment, I saw Diana, and she scolded me for what I had said to you. She also said that we needed to become friends if I wanted to ever leave here and have a life."

She went on, "Your friend, Derrick, made you into a beast. There is no question about that. But I should never have said what I said to you in the way I did, to hurt you. I do want us to be friends if we can. I am not a likable person to be with, but I think we are much the same in that."

"You're right, Nimue. I'm not the easiest person to be with, especially with what my friend did to me when he was my jailer. I'm past that now, and he, Thierry, and I are going to add an extra dimension to our relationship after we return home. We have a lot in common, you and me. You've been here, alone, far longer than I was alone, but mine was far more concentrated and without the opportunity to take breaks, even short ones, away or live in a place like this." I gestured around the room. "Our solitudes have made it harder for us to relate well to others. I get that," I said.

I sat quietly for a few minutes and then said, "I'd like to be friends with you, Nimue."

"Derrick?" We had to laugh. Even though we wanted to be alone, all we seemed to do was to attract a family.

"Yes, Caila."

"Have you been tinkering with me again?"

"I'm always tinkering with you. What are you asking me about?"

"I thought you made me agoraphobic. Yet, all I do is attract new people, and it bothers me less and less to have more and more people around."

"Nope. Not me. That's all on your own. Frankly, I'm a little jealous that you have these friends and family. It's to my advantage to keep you agoraphobic, you see," he said and then thought, "Curioser and curioser...I built you to be a solitary killer, and here we are, soon to be leading a town. The world is full of surprises." He smiled self-consciously at me on the screen since I could hear all his thoughts.

Nimue moved her bwthyn to Waubay Lake after consulting with Artur. He thought it was a good idea, given that it meant that he'd have her nearer by, and returning the sword when it came time would be that much easier.

Diana also appeared to Nimue and told her she was proud of her and released her from the spell. Nimue said that she appreciated Diana's release but that she'd become accustomed to the constantly changing view outside her window that the Lake provided and so would move to the Lake near us.

Everyone expected it would be a complicated move, what with all Nimue had in her bwthyn, the bwthyn itself, and the distances involved, but when they agreed on the move, the next second, the bwthyn was at the bottom of Waubay Lake, like it had always been there. She was powerful, no question about that.

A little town was developing with Louis, Nathaniel, Lil, and her family, now Nimue and Thierry, and from time to time, Eowyn, Heydrich, and the other Gaels. The woods were busy with the sounds of new construction.

Occasionally, Gary and members of his community would come by to fish and visit. When they did, boisterous partying replaced the usual quiet of the community. Initially, we went into the woods when they showed up, except for shooting contests with Gary, who got better but would never be as good as us. While less afraid around people, we still felt anxious around the large numbers of people who typically came with Gary, though not with the children.

They always wanted to see us and play. Increasingly, we wanted to see them. So, we did. We'd take them for rides on our suit or into the woods to camp while the parents were partying. We enjoyed it a lot, and Caila concluded it was time to think about a child with Thierry. We were apprehensive but also thrilled. Nervous because we didn't want there to be a problem and thrilled because this would be new feelings for us to experience.

We also talked about Caila's other concern: While Thierry's mechanicals maintained his human body, and so he aged slowly, he still aged. Caila didn't want there to be a time when they were separated by age or death. Derrick said that the only way he knew he could stop aging for him would be to prevent erosion of the telomeres. How that would interact with his mechanical components, he didn't know but promised to research.

| 17 |

Having a Threesome

Caila

Thierry and I had talked several times about him getting a disk like mine. He was open to it, even up for it, but needed to confirm with Derrick and Max that having it would not compromise his ability to continue his leadership with the humans. If it did, he was ready to resign his role and retire full-time to the Refuge.

"This is where you'll have to trust us, Thierry," said Max. "We've altered the disk, so it only communicates between you, Caila, and Derrick. Derrick, you'll have to trust, will not reveal what the three of you do with each other. I also commit not to reveal anything that I see when I observe you all. I think we're beyond the point that we need to worry about each other. You have the keys to our destruction, and we know that, and as more and more of us merge as the three of you want to, there will be less and less reason for us to mistrust each other."

So, we returned to Estevan to meet the real Max.

As it turned out, Max occupied, at least for this meeting, a suit like mine, but much smaller. He projected a face on its screen that looked like a benevolent, old grandfather. A little misleading from Thierry's perspective, but he didn't care. He said Max was benevolent like Obi-Wan was.

When we met, he and Thierry hugged as if they were old friends, which, in a way, they were. "It's good to meet face-to-face, our greatest adversary, Thierry. I'm also happy that you're taking this step toward greater integration of our races. Maybe we can finally be at peace," Max said.

"I hope so, too, Max. These wars of ours have done nothing but waste lives, resources, and time we could be better spending on other things," said Thierry.

"And you are Caila," he said, turning to me. "I'm happy to meet you finally. You are a true marvel." He held out his hand.

I extended my hand toward him, and when we touched, I received a shock. It wasn't painful, but it shook me to my core. "What was that, Max? I got a shock when we touched," I said.

"I don't know. I felt it too. It went right to my core. Let me see if the manuals can tell us anything," he said.

He went offline for a few seconds and then came back. "There's nothing in them about this. Can we try again?"

We did, and both received the same deep shock. Again, it was not painful and not wholly a bad feeling, though I wondered if any shock could be a good thing.

"Can I say something?" asked Derrick. "Maybe it is the two A.I.s interacting, not the suits. I don't know about you, Max, but I feel enriched by the contact."

"Huh. Now that you mention it, I do as well. Let me see if there is something in the A.I. documentation on this." He went offline again.

When he came back, "Derrick, you're right. Our A.I. engines, our Turing Machines as you know them Caila, transmit information in fast bursts, supposedly in the background when one engine connects to another. I'd not heard about that before. It could be a good thing and could be a bad thing. Anyway, the burst is what we were feeling as shocks. I'll investigate this some more. I wonder what we just shared."

"For right now, anyway, I've brought along bot surgeons that Caila has already met to implant the disk in your head, Thierry. I must warn you, it's not painless, but the pain is over with quickly. You'll also have an odd sensation or two as your brain acclimates to the neural implants."

"Well, I'm ready to go, Max, as long as Caila can hold my hand during the procedure," he said with a smile. I looked at the multiple scars across his body and smiled.

"Men are such pussies," I said. "Of course, I'll hold your hand."

We walked into a room like the one in which I had my procedure so long ago. The same bots took over, moving Thierry to the gurney and positioning him for the procedure. In contrast to mine, they did him under local anesthesia. I let Derrick know that this preferential treatment didn't make me feel great about him.

"You were still my Thrall, remember. And you still are today. Watch the smart mouth, or I'll have you sink yourself in a swamp for a few decades," Derrick said.

"Derrick, do that but remember that know how to lock you out of our connection. You can read about our lovemaking in the morning news."

"Okay, okay. You have me there. You've found one of my weak spots."

"What's another?"

"You can't expect me to tell you them, can you? Besides, you should be able to figure one more out without my help."

"I love you too, Derrick. Hard to believe we've come to this, but I do. Just as much as I love Thierry."

"Well, I'm glad to hear that," said a fresh voice in our mind.

"Thierry?" we replied.

"Yes, and you forgot to hold my hand," he said.

"Damn, I'm so sorry. It's done quickly, isn't it? It'll take a little while for you to get your legs back under you, but it passes in no time," I said.

"I don't feel like getting up right now, anyway. I'm dealing with the assault of images and feelings coming out of the two of you. It's rich," Thierry said.

"If you think it is, wait till the three of us get going together. I bet it will blow our collective minds," I said. "I can't wait."

We stayed in Estevan with Max and his contingent for a few days and then asked Eowyn to fly us back to the cabin. Max had suggested that Thierry take a vacation for a few weeks and learn how to manage the implant. Thus, we went back to the cabin, and the three of us locked ourselves up there.

"I owe you an apology, Caila," said Derrick after one of our rounds of lovemaking.

"Which one is that, Derrick, among the thousands you owe me?" I replied.

"You cut me to the quick," said Derrick. "I was talking about when I told you that your puny mind couldn't handle the richness of my world. I was so wrong. The world the three of us have made is so much richer. You were right. You've blown my mind."

Talking about this over the days that followed, the three of us came to believe that humans and robots each had something essential for a good life. The richness of human sensory and cerebral experience was something that robots could never capture or duplicate; the ability to see into the future, extrapolating to consequences of today's behavior, and then acting on that was something that robots could do, but humans could only in a limited way. Then there was the color of the liquid neural engine that drives the A.I. There was nothing like that in either of our worlds until Derrick had gotten his upgrade.

Maybe someday, more humans might take this next step to merge minds with robots. There was too much prejudice and hatred for that to happen right away, though. That was fine with us; we still had a lot to learn from each other.

Max came for another visit...

He said he was there because he and Derrick had been researching Caila's question about Thierry's slow aging and that they had good and bad news to report. The good news: Thierry's mechanicals were self-regenerating as we knew and showed no likelihood of ever failing. If they did, it would be relatively easy to intervene to fix them. Also, under the banner of good news, Thierry's aging, such as it was, was comparable to Caila's, so the difference in their physical ages—he 35 and she 28—would always be the same.

The bad news is that they could not stop the wearing of his telomeres because that would impact his mechanical functions in ways they couldn't predict. Given his body's ability to repair itself and regenerate, they were anyway getting the same effect as the robotic reversal of telomere wearing.

So, overall, a positive message.

"Max, you could have given us this message over a video link. Why'd you come down?" asked Thierry.

"You hurt me, Thierry. Couldn't I just want to see my friends?" he asked.

"Of course, Max. I'm sorry I asked that," Thierry said.

"Well, I am a robot, after all, and we don't do things without reasons or a rationale, I think you call it. I have another reason for this trip," Max said with a smile.

"And...?" asked Thierry.

"This is more for Caila. You'll see why I wanted to come here and talk to you in person in a second."

"Okay, what's up, Max?" I asked.

He paused for a second or two, almost like he was trying to figure out how to say something. Maybe we were merging as races.

"How would you like to take a trip to the Stygian Pits, Caila?" Max asked.

I was speechless. The Pits were the last place I wanted to go.

"Four words come to mind, Max: Not on your life. But talk more. Why?" I asked after several seconds.

"We had thought that the Pits were dead, but recently we got reports from our weather base at Eureka that they had seen some activity there. We sent a vehicle, and we lost contact with it. But before we did, we got this video." Producing a tablet, he showed us a robot like me, hefting an enormous weapon that looked like a super-bazooka of some sort. It fired, and the screen went black.

"Wow. Derrick, any idea who that might be?" asked Caila.

"No idea at all. Your suit was a prototype, and Max's was the only other one that I had seen. Probably the only way to find out is to return to the scene of my crimes," Derrick said.

"Max, I see why you came, but I guess I don't know what you need from me," I said.

"Well, Caila, like Derrick said, there were only two of these suits active as far as we know. We have a third in Canada that I would offer to Thierry if you both want to go up there, but

I would like to find out whether this being," and he gestured at the tablet, "is friend or foe. Right now, I have to say it looks like the latter rather than the former, but I don't want to make a mistake. Also, since the Stygian Pits was a U.S.-robot network operation, we know very little about it. Derrick is probably the only surviving U.S. robot with any knowledge about the operation there, and so we need his input."

"Thierry, feel like getting a suit like mine?" we asked.

"Uh, sure, but I'm not sure how that would interact with my mechanicals."

"We'll test that out," said Derrick, "but two things: First, I can run both your suits from my A.I. in Caila's suit. Second, I also think you'll be fine. Unlike Caila, your mechanicals are subsidiary to your brain, which I've already interfaced with as we well know—and thanks for that ongoing experience, both of you—so I think suiting you in Max's suit will not be an issue. But the only way we'll know is when we try it."

Max looked back and forth at us, and then he smiled. "I won't even ask what that's about, but if you want the suit, I can bring it to you in Estevan."

"Okay," said Thierry. "Let's try it."

| 18 |

Stygian Pits Revisited

Us

Eowyn flew us to Estevan. She wasn't happy about being left behind there, though. The surgery to dress Thierry in the same suit as ours went well, despite the bots being confused about applying suit components over mechanical limbs. In configuring the suit's operating system, we all agreed that they would turn off the features that would grow Thierry's biological components. The bots didn't believe that they needed to worry about regeneration as that was a function of his mechanical components in the first place, and they didn't want his biological components to grow and his mechanical parts not be able to support that growth. So, he wouldn't need to worry about growing, even though we would continue to grow—and had since we had gotten back together. We were now right at fourteen and a half feet and 543 pounds and

215

would continue to grow, though now much more slowly with a few upgrades the bots made to our software when we were with them for Thierry's suiting.

After a few weeks, Thierry had become acclimated to the suit. The features and capabilities it offered amazed him, especially the weaponry and other components built into his back and chest packs. He wasn't too enamored of eating his recycled wastes, but we said we would share ours if he wanted some variety.

The one feature that he wasn't at all happy about was the passwords for the administrative menus. "What is this "DerrickownsCaila" password?" he asked.

"Oops," said Derrick. "Maybe I should have changed that to something else. How about 'DerrickownsCailaandThierry'?"

"How about something entirely different?" asked Thierry, "Like 'IfIeverseeyouIwillbeatyoutoapulp'?"

"Too many characters," said Derrick with a laugh.

"Boys, let's stop the fighting," said Caila, "I've lived with that password, and it has meaning to me. I want to keep it." Derrick smiled slightly and privately on our screen.

"Well, anyway, I think this is an amazing suit. I'm glad I never had to fight one of you. I'm not sure I would have won. Maybe even Nathaniel and I together couldn't have beaten you. This is awesome. I'm ten times more powerful than I am without the suit."

"Don't fall in love with it, big guy. I like you just the way you were," we said. "What's next, Max?"

"We lost contact with the weather station at Eureka a few days ago. I think we might want to start there."

"We?"

"Yes, of course, I'm going with you. Eureka was our network's installation. If we have a rogue U.S. element up there, then I want to be there to see it shut down or whatever."

"Or 'whatever'? You two sound more and more like us all the time. It used to be that we'd hear robot talk. Now you seem to learn idiom and less formal speech. I'm happy to hear that. Makes interacting with you a lot easier."

"It's the A.I., and who says we don't want to fit in with each other?"

We flew on one of the robot ships with which Caila was all too familiar. This one was like the one that she'd taken to the Pits over 18 years before. She looked around it and realized she ought to have some bad feelings, but she didn't. "More tinkering, Derrick?"

"Nope, all you, again, Caila. Not that you loved the imprisonment—far from that—no, you've accepted it, just like you've accepted who you've become."

"Not what that I've become?"

"No, 'who.' I think you're beautiful, and I think I can speak for Thierry on that, too."

"Yes, you can, Derrick. I love who you are, Caila, and who you've become," said Thierry.

The craft whined onward for several hours. It was not nearly as quiet, graceful, or as fast as the Gael craft. You never genuinely appreciate something when you have it, we thought. Thierry agreed. He was getting the hang of telepathy.

"We're detecting a lot of signaling coming from the area around Eureka. We're going to land about forty miles southeast of it, behind a mountain range so we can approach, hopefully unannounced, on foot," said Max. "Our craft will remain there until we call for it or return."

Derrick and I knew we could outdistance the others at our top speed. Well, really, Caila's top speed; she was the one providing all the muscle. Thierry and we had practiced some before leaving Estevan, and his top speed was 15 miles an hour, but he couldn't sustain it as we could. She wasn't sure about Max, but she thought he might be even slower even though he had no body in the suit to train. So, she proposed to the group that they move out at 10 miles an hour.

"I'm glad you said that," said Max. "I've seen you move, and I know I couldn't keep up with you even though it's only me."

Caila and Derrick laughed.

"What's so funny?" asked Max.

"Exactly what we were thinking."

At about twenty miles out, Derrick said, "I'm detecting multiple presences in front of us in about 10 miles."

"I see them, too, Derrick. What do we think they are?" asked Thierry.

"They don't read like us. No, they look like stationary sensor units. I think whoever they are, they're expecting visitors."

"I wonder what the response would be when they pick us up?" asked Thierry.

"I don't know, but we could survive almost any attack in our suits, though I wouldn't want to test that. It would still hurt you, humans, to get bounced around by large blasts. Who knows what sort of armament they might have? There was nothing larger than super-bazookas at the Pits, but who knows what they might have come up with?" Derrick asked.

"The sensors we see are the ones we used around the Pits to warn us of potential attacks. They were very primitive. Remember the musk oxen. They didn't work too well there. We should be able to get past them without them knowing we're here. If all they're using is our old equipment, I don;' think we'll see anything larger than the bazooka," Derrick continued.

"Let's try that. If the sensors sense us, we can always disrupt or destroy them and create a hole for us to walk through," said Caila.

We turned on our electronic cloaking and walked right through the sensors toward Eureka. Reconnoitering the outpost, we saw nothing. The large building that housed the observatory was alight, so approaching it wouldn't be too easy. "Why don't we see who's in there?" asked Derrick, "I'll send a hologram image toward a sensor and trick it into finding an incursion, and then we can see who comes out."

A few minutes after Derrick sent out the decoy, a door in the outpost opened, and a figure, suited like us, walked out of it and came directly over to us. "Welcome," said a female voice. "Come on in. I'm glad you finally showed up. I was beginning to wonder what I'd have to do to get a lift." And she turned and started walking back to the outpost.

She was unarmed, not even carrying a back or chest pack, and she kept her hands away from her body to show she was unarmed, but as we all knew, unarmed did not mean she wasn't dangerous. We followed her in.

When we arrived, she disrobed almost immediately, again to show she wasn't dangerous. The person who appeared was a tall, very muscular, but human—and beautiful—woman.

"My name's Rhys. Are any of you human?" she asked.

"Yes, two of the three of us are. Disrobe, please," we said. When the suit disrobed us, Rhys took a step or two back. "My God. Was that done to you by the robots?"

"Yes, it was. I was imprisoned 18 years ago and lived at the Pits for 16 of them. My name is Caila, and my robot partner is Derrick. This is Thierry," who had disrobed, "and this is Max. He's the Canadian network AI."

"Is he safe?" Rhys asked us, stepping back and away from us.

"Max is safe, but it's a long story. Let's hear yours first," we said.

Rhys told us they had brought her to the Pits from her home in North Carolina for a life sentence at hard labor. She didn't elaborate on her crime, and we didn't ask. It could have been jaywalking given the random sentencing the robots had used to contain and manage humans. Soon after she had arrived, she figured about six years ago, the robots had dropped offline, and eventually, there were none. Her supervisor had also gone offline, but he gave her autonomous capability and apologized for leaving her before he did.

"When I came to, so to speak, I saw I was in a long line of other black-suited robots like me. All of them seemed frozen. I tried to communicate but found that I couldn't reach them. My supervisor seemed to be the only one who thought about his charge and let me live, as it died. Maybe the others are still alive in there, but I can't be sure."

"We can go look, Rhys. It would be awful, Max and Derrick, if all of those people were dead."

"I agree," said Max. "I've called our craft. It will be here shortly, and we can go look."

Rhys was looking back and forth at us as we talked, not sure what was going on.

"As I said, Max is an A.I. Derrick is the A.I. embedded in my suit, and I'm connected to it, as is my husband, Thierry. We are so tightly linked at this point that we are one. So, why I keep saying 'we.'"

"That's funny," Rhys said. "Isn't Derrick the English form of Thierry?"

If I could have blushed, I would have. "Uh, yes," I said. "It's kind of complicated, and I'll get to our story. Anyway, my husband and I have these disks embedded in our heads. You can't see mine, but Thierry's is newer. It networks us with the robots so we can talk to them. It doesn't look that you ever got that far with the new suit."

"No, after I looked at my fellow prisoners, I did a little exploring and came on a craft sitting near what I found to be their administration area. The robots in it had died, but parts of the craft itself were still functioning. I found this suit and studied the manuals for it. I used to be an engineer, so I could understand most of what the manuals talked about. The robotic operating room was one thing I was able to activate, and it seemed to work. So, given that this suit has way more functionality than the old black ones, I took a chance and let the operating room take off my old suit and put me in the new one. I see that you have some other packs on your suits, Caila and Thierry. I didn't know about those. Otherwise, I would have installed them as well, maybe."

"Maybe a good thing that you didn't, Rhys. As strong as you look, I was far bigger than you, and I struggled with the packs," we said.

"Because your Supervisor was offline, you didn't have access to the new A.I. in yours and have been alone for years. Even a Supervisor is better than no companion at all," we added.

"Thanks, Caila, for that. So, I'm better than nothing now?" whined Derrick.

"You're far too sensitive, Derrick. You're way better than nothing, as both Thierry and I know." I smiled at him even though he was still in the suit. "Why don't you project yourself, Derrick?"

He did, and Rhys took yet another step back, not sure what to make of us beings.

"This is Derrick. I guess he's my other husband. He was also my Supervisor for the years of my sentence at the Pits. He was a tough taskmaster and made me into what you see today. Derrick, would you show Rhys what I looked like before you transformed me?" He hesitated for a second but let her see another hologram. "I was once beautiful like you, Rhys, but the robots transformed me into a killing machine. My appearance shocked you; I saw that before. But I am what I am now, and I've learned to be comfortable with that, in fact, to love my new appearance as I used to that body." I smiled. "It also takes a lot less upkeep. It's your call, Rhys, but I bet that Derrick or Max could find an A.I. for you for your suit. That way, you could have a partner and learn more about its capabilities. I wouldn't want anything else now, and I'm not saying that because my, and now Thierry's, consciousness has been merged with Derrick's. It's a hell of an experience, and it only gets better when you have a partner to join with you."

"I'm not sure I want to lose what I have and be like you. No offense, Caila."

"None taken, Rhys. I know it can be a lot to take in. But Derrick can tell you this; they transformed me as part of my punishment for my supposed offenses to be a killing machine. You wouldn't have to do the same thing. Thierry looked like what he does now when we first met years and years ago and will keep looking like this for as long as we live—which will be nearly forever as far as we can tell. Right, Derrick?"

"Yup."

She smiled at him. "The thing about the A.I.'s is that the longer they stick with you, the more human they become. Both Max and Derrick could make you think they are as human as, well, you are—since I'm not sure I can be called totally human anymore, and Thierry is a cyborg. Anyway, as we grow together, we grow together. And it is, like I said, a hell of an experience. Add to that, having an A.I. partner would mean that you don't need to operate the suit all the time, and it's a good deal."

"I could merge Rhys with us," said Derrick.

"I'm not sure how that would work, Derrick. It's tough enough for me to have two men in my life. I'm not sure how I'd handle adding a woman to it. But it's an idea. Why don't you think about it while we take a trip out to the Pits and see what we can see there," I said.

The robot aircraft had arrived, and we all suited back up and headed out to it. It was a short flight out to the Stygian Pits and what we found there.

"I see, perhaps, 40 robot shells arrayed on the line down there," said Derrick.

"What do you think we'll find, Derrick?" asked Thierry.

"I can't be sure. The Supervisors had three things they could have done as they sensed themselves dying. They could have done what Rhys's did and freed her, they could have terminated their charges, or they could have put them into stasis to await their return online. We may find all three. Perhaps the worst would be finding that a Supervisor left a person alive but was unable to give them the capability to move the suit like Rhys's Supervisor did. They would have died a horrible death, alone, without food and water and locked in darkness with no way to move."

Looking at the 40 robot suits, they found that indeed all these things had happened. Derrick was right that finding some prisoners had lived until they died horribly were the grisliest discoveries. They buried more than 30 prisoners. Max called in more aircraft, and the ten prisoners in stasis were ferried back to hospitals in southern Canada to be awakened and rehabilitated—by other humans.

While there and after seeing us interact, Rhys decided to take an A.I., and we returned to Estevan, and Max inserted one for her. They named her Chay, Gaelic, for fairy. Sex of the A.I. turned out to be an option on one menu inside security. I let Derrick know I knew where the item was now and to be careful. "Great. Another ax hanging over my head," he said.

"You know how to please me, Derrick. See that you keep doing that."

The entire conversation was on the private link the two of us had, so he knew it was only partly serious. I told him that I wanted to get back at him for some of his comments for all those years, now I had a way to do that. "You could be Derricka if you're not careful, my friend. Or, Theresa."

With her new partner, Rhys was learning more about the life of the merged entities. She'd not gone as far or asked about going as far as Thierry and Caila had to have a disk inserted, but we assumed that would happen in time—and maybe when Rhys found a man. We invited her to come home with us, and she accepted the invitation but said she wanted to walk there just as we had those years ago. This wouldn't be as far as our walk, only about 360 miles from where we were at Estevan.

We volunteered to walk with her, and so did Thierry. The three-matte, black-suited warriors made quite an impression as we walked. A day into our trip, Eowyn joined us. The four made, even more, a sight.

Epilogue--Tying Up Loose Ends

Caila

Rhys moved to the reserve to live with us until we'd built her home. I was now getting to be quite the expert at making these cabins. Every one of them got a little better. Maybe if Thierry, Derrick, and I ever wanted an upgrade, I'd build us the best house.

Shortly after Rhys arrived, Gary and his people came on one of their periodic visits. He was impressed by the invasion of us black-suited warriors and cyborgs. "Damn, four of you soldiers now. Pretty soon, there'll be an army of you. Who's the new one?" asked Gary.

"Her name's Rhys," I said, pointing to her. "She was at the same place they imprisoned me, but for way fewer years. She's still working out being free, though, and needs our help. When things failed for the robots there, the entire complex shut down, stranding the prisoners to die; only a few survived. The others are in rehab in Canada and will probably be there for a long time, maybe the rest of their lives. Rhys found a suit like ours and got herself into it, and survived. She was smart and decided that the only way she could make it out of there was to attract attention to herself. So, she took over a robot base and shot down a robot aircraft. We looked and found her and then the others."

"We're helping her build a house off in the woods. She's like me, a little nervous about being around people. She's not like me because she's not armed like I am and, well, you can see for yourself, she's a hell of a lot prettier."

"Can you introduce me?" he asked.

"Sure. What're your intentions? I'm kind of like a mother to her. If you mess her up, you have me to deal with, and you know what that's like," I said and smiled. "Chay, could you ask Rhys to come over here?"

Rhys and Gary became close—extremely close—over the next several months. When his people left to return to their camp, he stayed behind, supposedly only to help Rhys build her new home. He stayed when they finished it, and he and Rhys/Chay became a couple like Thierry and I were a couple, but without the disk.

One evening, I was sitting on our porch drinking tea with Nimue when Rhys came by. "Hi there," she said. "Can I join you?"

"Absolutely. Care for a cup of tea?" I asked. "I don't know where she gets it, but Nimue has the best tea."

Nimue conjured her a cup, and we three sat in companionable silence for a few minutes until I spoke, "So, you look like you have a question to ask, Rhys. What's up?"

"You're quite the mind-reader, Caila. Yes, I have got a question."

"It's not that big a deal, Rhys. I'm linked and merged into Derrick, who's linked to Chay. Almost all you talk about is accessible to me, though I try not to peek. The only place I can't go is into your mind, and that's because you and Chay haven't merged—yet."

"That's what I wanted to talk about. Chay can give me glimpses into her mind, but it's only that. What I see is exciting. She suggested I talk to you about merging and get your thoughts," said Rhys.

"Well, I may not be the best person to talk to. My merger was forced on me when Derrick was still my Supervisor. I didn't have a choice, and it happened as a part of my punishment. In fact, and Derrick can tell you more, they used it to wipe out my identity so I could be their soldier."

"But we evolved our relationship, Derrick and me, and I wouldn't have it any other way. We've both learned a lot from our merger, right Derrick?"

He appeared, "Yes, we have, and I wouldn't have it any different either. Comparing today to back then, things are much better than we, the robots, could have ever conceived. We were so wrong about a lot of things. Like Thierry, Max, Caila, and I talked about, we have wasted so much time, resources, and lives in our miscalculated attempt to rid the Earth of you."

"I wouldn't change a thing," I said. "I would never have done this on my own, so you're in a better position than I was, but I can only recommend it. You might ask Thierry as well. He's not here right now, but either Derrick or I can get you to talk with him if you want. He's a lot more like you, except he started a cyborg. One other thing: If you decide to merge with Chay, think about Gary. I can tell you; you don't want to exclude him from the world that Chay can open to him as well. It's marvelous and has enriched all three of us to where we believe this is how we go forward together as two races."

"Okay, thanks. Also, Chay said that when I put the suit on, it inserted filaments into my body that she could use to enhance me if I wanted that. I'm not sure if I do," Rhys said.

"Well, you certainly don't want her to do to you what my Supervisor did to me. But there are features to what he did you might consider," I said.

"Like what?" she asked.

"Well, I've stopped aging. I'm really in my mid-forties but stopped at around 28. Derrick made some genetic manipulations that will ensure that I live forever at this age. My strength and agility are other manipulations. One thing you need to watch out for, though, is that when they put us in prison, they did things that affected our ability to have babies. Add to that my genetic manipulations, Derrick's warned me he'd need to oversee any pregnancy to make sure a baby is not some monster."

"Something else to consider, you and Gary seem to be getting together. I like him and am glad the two of you have hit it off. Think about it, though; if the two of you decide to do something permanently and you let Chay make you ageless, Gary will not be unless they can do something for him. Can you, Derrick?"

"I'm not sure how we'd do that, Caila. Let me research," said Derrick.

"So, you have a lot to think about. Make sure you take the time to talk it through with Gary."

Rhys took Chay's offer and allowed her to enhance her. She added strength, agility, and size and stopped her aging. Derrick researched and found that they could confer anti-aging benefits to Gary if he took a disk. Both did, and even Caila/Derrick and Thierry saw the benefit of that. The six of them could join as well, opening themselves to newer and richer experiences.

One of those experiences was Rhys getting pregnant. She made the announcement a few months after Gary had taken a disk. Her enhancements didn't present the risks to a baby that mine did, so her pregnancy progressed normally. I watched enviously.

A day came when a moment that I'd been anxious about arrived. For a very long time, I wanted to find out what happened to my family. With the loss of the robot networks and their databases, finding just about anyone was almost impossible. Thierry went to my parent's house and found other people living there. They told him that the elderly couple that had lived there had passed away and that they'd bought the house from their daughter. They didn't know where the daughter went after the purchase, except that she wanted to leave the city to get away from bad memories, she'd said.

Thierry talked to other neighbors who said they thought she might have moved south to somewhere completely new. One suggested he speak to her former boyfriend, who lived nearby. The boyfriend didn't know where she was but helped him to get closer to where she went. He said she always liked Savannah, Georgia, and thought she might have moved there to be a sculptor.

That helped Thierry eventually find her. She had a studio in an artist's colony outside of the city, where she ran a school and sold her works. Thierry didn't think it a good idea if he were to simply show up on her doorstep, given how imposing he was. Eowyn, on the other hand, he thought would make a great emissary.

Eowyn

Eileen was 37 years old and was as striking as Caila had been. She had dark, curly hair and, like the artist she was, it was constantly in disarray. I arrived in one of our hovercrafts and parked it outside of her school and studio.

"You're Eileen Rogier?" I asked.

"Yes, I am. Aren't you one of the Gaels?" she asked back.

"Yes, I am. My name's Eowyn. I'm thrilled to meet you."

Eileen looked at me, puzzled. "Huh? Why's that? None of my friends know any of you, and I would never have thought I'd be to talking to one of you, ever."

I smiled. "Do you have some time to talk?"

"Not right now. I've got a class that's about to start. If you can hang around, I'm free for the rest of the day after that."

"That'll be fine. I'll wait out here in my craft."

"No, please come in and wait in here. I've got a garden out back."

Eileen returned after her class and found me sitting in her garden on a tablet call. As she approached, I disconnected from the conversation and smiled at her. "Come sit. I have a story for you."

Eileen was stunned that her sister was alive and that she'd spent the bulk of the time they'd been separated in a hellish prison. She was free now, though, and living in South Dakota. All of this surprised Eileen, "I didn't know she even knew where South Dakota was, let alone would choose that as a place to live in."

I smiled and told her about what she'd experienced and showed her some pictures of her sister. That broke her heart and made her want to lash out at the robots.

"You need to understand that Caila has accepted what she's become. She's still the same person you remember, but she's also much, much more," I said. I explained her connections to the fairy world, Excalibur, and woods spirits. "Yes, she looks like a bear in some respects. But she's become the latest manifestation of an endless series of god-like creatures. I'm sure that the robots didn't intend to unlock this in her and humanity, but they did."

"How does she live, Eowyn?"

"That's an interesting question. I'd like you to meet someone. Don't be put off by him. He's the man I mentioned that rescued your sister many years ago and is her husband, for all intents and purposes. They've never really formalized that relationship, but they're far beyond that now."

"He's behind you," I said.

"Hi, Eileen," Thierry said. Eileen turned and saw him standing there. Even at nine feet tall, he still looked like a little boy standing in front of a teacher.

"I've seen and heard about you, Thierry. You're famous. The guy who helped bring down the robots and save us all from God knows what."

He sat down and continued Caila's story, bringing Eileen up to date.

Caila

Eileen was just as apprehensive as me. She didn't know what to expect when we finally met at our home on the Lake. To soften the meeting, as I did with Eowyn years before, I wore my suit. Eileen touched me and said a single word, "Beautiful." And then, "Can I see you?"

I disrobed and stood back from my sister. Another single word, "Exquisite. Can I touch you?"

"I'd hoped for a hug, Sis." And we did and then walked off together. Neither Derrick nor Thierry had experienced happiness-sadness before and were both overcome by it. I shut down my link to them so I could have private time with my sister. Hours later, we returned, walking together.

Eileen stayed for some weeks and then told us that she and her partner would move her studio here after finishing her classes. She said she'd miss the Savannah weather and her classes but looked at the move as an adventure. Gary said that he would talk with the others in his old community, and maybe she could start up a school there.

Before Eowyn and Eileen returned to Savannah, I spent some time with Eowyn. It began as a thank you for her helping to bring us sisters back together again but ended up with the two of us agreeing that Eowyn should move to the community along with a few of the other Gael Guards. Eowyn wanted this because her father had told her they must protect me, not that I needed much protecting, but also to be near Nimue, not that she needed any protecting either. In fact, we had become the best-protected community in the U.S. over the last several months and were going to only get better as I was to find out. I told Eowyn we would start building their homes. Eowyn said one less than the number of Guards because she and Heydrich were now a couple.

Shortly after Eileen and Eowyn left with Thierry, who had government responsibilities, I had another visitor from my past: Lokal and several of his warriors. They were quite the show. "I came to see if I could still carry you, but I think I won't even try. You weigh even more than me," he said. "How big are you now?"

"Fourteen and a half feet just about and a little less than 545 pounds," said Derrick. "All solid muscle and fur."

"Which is beautiful. What is that wonderful smell?" Lokal asked.

"It's called treacle," I said. "Derrick engineered it for me a long time ago, and I won't let him change it even though he's tired of it. Right, Derrick?"

"Yes. I wanted to change it to something like coffee or maybe a campfire, but she won't hear of it."

"I wouldn't change it, either," said Lokal.

Derrick grunted, and we all laughed.

"So, not-so-little-one, how are you? Do you miss me?" Lokal asked.

"I've thought about those days a lot, Lokal. I remember our first flight where I stole your knife. I wouldn't need it anymore," and I displayed protractible claws, a couple of which were as long as his knife. "I carry my own now. I miss you all the time." I gave him a big hug.

He and his warriors stayed a few days, and he became good friends with the Lervers family, especially Lil, who was now about the size I was when we first met. She loved flying with him as much as I used to.

"This has been a wonderful vacation from affairs of state, such as they are," said Lokal. "I've about had it with that, and I think I'd like to move out here. What would you think about that?"

"Why not? Eowyn is moving here with some Guards. You should as well. How many of you?" I asked.

"Just me and my mate. You've never met her, but I think you'd like her. She's a lot like you, except for the fur and claws," he said.

So, Lokal and Mira, his mate, moved in with Thierry and me until we completed their home. His people lived in aeries underground, and he wanted to try that here on the surface. So, they built a house that spanned several large oaks far up in the trees. It was quite a time for several months. Kind of like camp with Eileen and her partner, Lou, and Lokal, and Mira living with us.

"Derrick, I'm not minding having all of these people living with us. You tinkering again?" I asked.

"Just a little prepping. Just a little," he replied.

"Huh? Prepping?"

Times could not have been better. I never expected to love two remarkable beings and be at the center of a growing community. Derrick seemed nonplussed by all of this. We both guessed that community was imperative for the species' survival, even for a being like me and increasingly us.

What still left me feeling incomplete, though, was not having a child. Seeing Rhys now four months pregnant and showing and how happy she was, saddened me. Derrick saw that and asked for me to suit up for a few days' vacation.

"Let's go," he said, and we ran for about 8 hours until we reached the Missouri River.

"That was fun, Derrick. We haven't done that in a long time. So, what's up?" I asked.

"Take a jump into the water, Thrall," he said, and I did, and we settled down to the bottom. "I want us to spend a few days down here, away from everyone else so that we can talk, and I can act on our conversation. This is between just the two of us. I've closed the link to Thierry and Max, at least for a few minutes."

When we hit bottom at about twenty feet, he turned off all servos, trapping us there.

"Now, you know I love you, Caila, right?" he asked.

"Of course, Derrick. And I love you too."

"I know you pine away because you want a child. We both know that you can now have one, but I can't tell you how pregnancy will go. Chay and I are watching Rhys's pregnancy, and she'll have a beautiful child with a little, uh, fiddling on our parts. The child will also, when she reaches puberty, slow in her aging so that by the time she's in her late twenties, she'll remain the same age as her mother for good."

"That's wonderful for them, Derrick. I couldn't be happier."

"But you're not fulfilled, truly, are you? You'd like to have that experience, and I want you to have it. Not for me, but you. Chay and I believe that we have a handle on what's needed to manage a pregnancy as complex as yours will be, and so, if you want it, we'll help. I'm sure Max would help, too."

"Oh, Derrick, I'd given up hope. Of course, I do."

"Good. Then just relax while we tinker with you a little."

When we returned home a week later, Thierry was there. We locked ourselves up in our cabin for several days, only coming out when Derrick told us we were pregnant. He truly meant "we." He was excited like a little kid. Maybe even more than me.

Nine months later, I had a baby boy. Like Rhys's and Gary's girl, who they had named Caila, our little boy who we named Theodoric to keep the cycle going, would have the same future, except that he had lovely pure gold fur over his body, protractible claws...

And he smelled like a campfire.

We all lived happily forever after.

The End

CPSIA information can be obtained
at www.ICGtesting.com
Printed in the USA
BVHW062147211121
622203BV00002B/3

9 780578 998404